"Something about all this doesn't add up."

Charity moved closer to the still-open front door. "You show up here uninvited, tackle me, tear up the place, then you say you want *us* to keep quiet about your family nickname?"

"Actually, I'd like you to keep my family quiet," Jason said. "That hasn't worked out too good for me, so far. They're one reason I came out here today."

"One reason?" The reticent redhead stepped into the shaft of light cast by the open door. "And the other reason would be?"

To pay a debt. To set everything right. To be your hero.

Each idea that popped into his head sounded hokier than the next. Finally he settled on the simple unvarnished truth as he believed it. "I came because you're here."

Books by Annie Jones

Love Inspired

April in Bloom
Somebody's Baby
Somebody's Santa
Somebody's Hero

Steeple Hill Café

Sadie-in-Waiting
Mom Over Miami
The Sisterhood of the
* Queen Mamas*

ANNIE JONES

Annie Jones, winner of the Holt Medallion for Southern Themed Fiction, and the *Houston Chronicle*'s Best Christian Fiction Author of 1999, grew up in a family that loved to laugh, eat and talk—often all at the same time. They instilled in her the gift of sharing through words and humor, and the confidence to go after her heart's desire (and to act fast if she wanted the last chicken leg). A former social worker, she feels called to be a "voice for the voiceless" and has carried that calling into her writing by creating characters often overlooked in our fast-paced culture—from seventy-somethings who still have a zest for life to women over thirty with big mouths and hearts to match. Having moved thirteen times during her marriage, she is currently living in rural Kentucky with her husband and two children.

Somebody's Hero
Annie Jones

Steeple
Hill®

Published by Steeple Hill Books™

STEEPLE HILL BOOKS

Steeple
Hill®

Recycling programs
for this product may
not exist in your area.

ISBN-13: 978-0-373-87520-7
ISBN-10:   0-373-87520-7

SOMEBODY'S HERO

Greater love hath no man than this, that a man lay down his life for his friends.
—*John* 15:13

For my heroes—my parents Alpha
and Maxine Shorter

Prologue

Four weeks to Heritage Days
Mt. Knott, South Carolina

Jason Burdett believed in God and prayer.

Jason believed that to understand a man's character, one needed to look at the choices that man made more than what he said.

Jason also believed he had been granted more than his share of grace and blessings.

And most of all, Jason believed this morning that if one more person called him Lucky Dawg, he'd forget his manners for a split second and sock that person square in the jaw.

He seated himself at the long table in the center of Josie's Home Cookin' Kitchen where the rest of his family sat waiting for him so they could say grace over their lunch.

"Here's to Lucky Dawg!" Josie Burdett, the six months pregnant wife of Jason's older brother, Adam, raised a frosty glass of milk.

Okay, Jason thought, the *second* person to call him that...

"To Lucky Dawg!" Every last person sitting at the Burdett table chimed in. The youngest of the brothers, a minister who didn't seem to mind being called Hound Dawg, actually howled out the name.

"Here's to the last of the pack of Burdett boys to remain a lone wolf," Burke, the eldest of the four brothers, nicknamed Top Dawg, bellowed.

"I'm not finished, y'all!" Josie stomped her foot, making her ponytail of golden curls bounce, then raised her glass again. "Here's to Lucky Dawg, our Heritage Days hero."

Hero? Jason cringed at the very word. He wanted to protest but knew it would be out of place and out of character. Jason did not argue with his family, even when they were dead wrong. "I'm just...you know..."

The phone in the office rang, the one Josie had to answer even though she'd closed the restaurant for an hour for this family gathering. She excused herself and the group politely held off attacking their meal until her return.

Jason used the moment to sweep his gaze over the faces surrounding him.

Conner Burdett, his father, had built an almost iconic snack cake business from a family recipe.

His brothers had all married and made their mark. Burke had formed a foundation to help the needy in the region, which he and Dora now ran. Adam had taken over the running of the family business, turned it around and made fans of the Carolina Crumble Pattie everywhere east of the Mississippi. He also had one son and another baby on the way. Cody had his church, his faith, his ministry and a lovely wife.

What did Jason have? A story everyone in town knew about escaping death as a kid? A wall of trophies and a bum knee from his college football days? The kind of looks—tall, tanned, unruly blond hair—that attracted his pick of pretty women? More money than he knew what to do with?

Oh, yeah, and a nickname that all of the other things only served to underscore. *Lucky Dawg.* As if nothing had come to him by hard work or diligence or intellect or even deservedness. Just dumb luck.

Jason did not even believe in luck.

Sure, he had a fancy title, Vice President of Special Projects. What a joke. Special Projects? It should have said, Jack-of-All-Trades, master of most everything but his own fate.

No, that would be too long.

If they really wanted to put the right title on the door of his office at the Carolina Crumble Pattie factory, they should put Fireman. Jason spent most of his days putting out fires. Correction. Putting out *other people's* fires.

Sounds like a job for…

"Lucky Dawg?"

Jason jerked his head up to see Josie standing in the doorway, her expression serious but not tense.

"I hate to bother you with us just about to eat and all…"

Jason tossed his napkin on the table and pushed his chair back hard and quick, making the legs scrape against the old but meticulously polished floor. "What do you need?"

"I wouldn't ask you. But that was Bingo Barnes and he was just driving by and…" She gave a nervous laugh. "He didn't think he should bother the police. It's not *that* kind of thing. But maybe…maybe it's nothing. It's probably nothing. But if anyone is going to check…"

"Josie, what is it?" Jason stood.

"Bingo just drove by Twin Cabins Lake and he thought he saw a kid trying to break into the main cabin nearest the road."

Twin Cabins Lake. Jason clenched his jaw. He hated that place.

And loved it.

But mostly, he hated himself for what it represented to him. The road not taken, as the famous poem said. The path that had led to his best friend's downfall.

That's why this time when his family had a request Jason had to say, "I'll go."

"Thanks!" Josie called after him, then in an obvious

attempt to lighten the moment, followed up sweetly with, "You're our hero!"

"Hero?" he murmured.

That word again.

This time Jason could not—would not—let it stand.

Hand to the door, he did not look back at the loving family who didn't seem to have the slightest clue who he really was. He simply exhaled and looked past his own reflection out onto the streets of Mt. Knott. For once, he spoke the truth for all to hear. "Don't you believe it, y'all. I'm a lot of things to a lot of people, but rest assured, I am nobody's hero."

Chapter One

Ten days to Heritage Days
Twin Cabins Lake

"**Y**ou cannot run away from me. You can't keep hiding." Jason's heart pounded. He could hardly swallow. "I've been sent out here four times now and have come away empty-handed each time."

You're our hero. Josie's teasing remark from two weeks earlier echoed in his thoughts as he stood on the porch contemplating something foolhardy.

He turned the knob to the right forcefully. The old fixture wrenched every joint and muscle from his wrist to his shoulder. He let go and flexed his fingers, shaking his arm. "Okay, a locked door might slow me down, but it's hardly going to stop me."

Jason rubbed his shoulder and regrouped again. He could do this.

Slightly built and quick-footed, always wearing a red hoodie that kept his face in shadow, the kid seen out at the lake time and again hadn't harmed anyone or stolen anything, as far as anyone could tell. There were no outward signs of vandalism. Just an unsettling presence that needed to be sorted out.

Jason shifted his boots to get some traction on the slanting old porch. As if somehow he *could* dispense with the "unsettling presence" out here. He found everything about Twin Cabins Lake unsettling.

The place held too much history.

Too much grief.

Too many times he had driven out here, sat by these still waters and wished that things had been different. He wished that years ago when his friend Sean had come to him with the wild idea to buy this land and reinvent the old fishing cabins as a family tourist retreat that he had...

Done what? To this day Jason couldn't say what would have been the right choice.

Jason looked out at the lake again. But what would it have cost them? Would their friendship have survived? Would they have ended up blaming and then resenting each other? Would things, ten years later, have really turned out so differently?

"Greater love hath no man than this, that a man would lay down his life for his friends." The thirteenth verse from John 15 replayed in Jason's mind, as it often did when he thought of Sean O'Clare.

Lay down his life? Jason couldn't even lay down his lifestyle. Sean had needed him once—counted on him—and Jason had failed.

Failed as a friend. Failed as a man of faith. Failed as a hero.

And now some creep was messing around with Sean's land, or what was left of it. He eyed the old door again.

"Did you hear me? I'm giving you to the count of three to come out or I'm coming in." How hard could it be for the best college football player to ever come out of Mt. Knott to break down this rickety old door?

Even if that football player was now over thirty years old and mostly a desk jockey.

Jason took a moment to figure his odds of success in breaking down the door. The two large cabins facing one another across the still, deep waters were mirror images of one another. They had been built in the 1920s as a summer getaway for Northern city dwellers. Sean had managed to sublet them out to someone who kept them going until about three years ago. About the time his parents had said Sean had taken a turn for the worse with his life choices. No one had stayed here since then.

The wooden door frame looked shoddy. The hinges had begun to rust. If he had to, Jason could force his way in.

"One."

He held his breath and listened.

"Two."

No response. Not even a shuffling of feet.

Maybe the kid had crawled out a back window and hightailed it to…to where? He glanced behind him.

Jason himself had helped Sean clear away the brush and ground cover between the buildings and the tall Carolina pines trees that formed a wall of seclusion from the dirt road beyond. No one who had gone into that cabin could come back out without showing themselves.

"Three."

Jason lowered his shoulder and aimed it at the door of the cabin using the skills that had earned him a football scholarship to the University of South Carolina. *Fourteen years ago.*

The door frame cracked, the hinges creaked and the door swung open. Jason felt every minute of those fourteen years in his muscles, nerves and tendons as he went tumbling forward, head down.

His eyes could not adjust fast enough to the darkness. A cobweb caught his arm and clung to his hair. A shaft of sunlight from the door slashed across but did not dispel the darkness. He pitched forward into that darkness, disoriented.

Wham!

He landed in a full sprawl on the floor and bit his tongue. When he opened his eyes, he found himself staring into a pair of dead eyes.

Dust from the red, green and tan braided rug

hung in the air around his head, but as it cleared he reconsidered.

Not dead eyes, *glass* eyes. Glass eyes set in the biggest big-mouthed bass he had ever seen. A stuffed bass, mounted on a plaque, its impressive jaws gaping. And stuffed inside that big mouth of that stuffed big-mouthed bass? A full set of human dentures.

Jason sneezed.

The fish did not offer so much as a "God bless you." Nor did anyone else.

"Kid must have gotten away," he grumbled to his newfound companion.

Another groan. His tongue hurt. His whole body hurt. His ego didn't exactly feel spiffy, either.

If he had been another kind of man, he probably would have cursed. Maybe picked up that plaque and turned that big-mouthed bass into a flying fish. But not Jason. He had a job to finish. He had to find that kid.

"Don't even think about it." A hiking boot came down on the back of his neck.

Cool, fresh, earthy-smelling mud smeared into his skin. It fell like moist cake crumbs into the blond hair that now hung over Jason's eyes.

"Stay right where you are." The low, growling voice quivered.

Jason's cheek chafed against the dirty rug. Kid didn't get away. Jason had to admire his grit. "Okay. Okay. Let's not get crazy here."

He could practically imagine the thought bubble

over the head of the dentured old bass telling him, *Too late. The crazy train pulled out of the station when you started talking to me.*

"Look, mister, you better not try anything or I'll…I'll…" The speaker bent down and plucked up the fish.

"You'll what? Beat me with the carp?" He laughed not because it was funny but because he hoped it would throw the fish-swinger off guard. Or should he say, off balance?

"It's not a carp, mister, it's a…"

Whomp!

Jason grabbed the kid's ankle and yanked. The floor shook from the impact when the kid's baggy jeans hit the dingy braided rug. More dust.

Jason knew to hold his breath.

The kid coughed then leaned forward, shoulders hunched, face hidden by the sweatshirt hood, gasping to get a deep breath.

Jason took advantage of the moment. He seized the kid's other ankle. One hard, sure twist and he flipped his assailant facedown with unexpected ease. Without stopping to think about that too much, Jason sat squarely on the pair of hiking boots, pinning the trespasser's lower body in place. He snagged first one wrist and then the other. He clamped them down in the small of the kid's back, which was smaller, he realized, than he had expected it to be.

An odd feeling sank like a stone in the pit of his

stomach. "Let's not let this get out of hand, here. If you promise to stay calm and cooperative, I'll—"

"Yes. I'll cooperate. Take anything." The rug muffled the voice but didn't slow the kid's words from pouring forth. "Take my money. Take my credit cards. Take my SUV. Only please, please don't—"

"Take?" Jason sat back on his heels, still restraining the intruder but with much less enthusiasm than he had a moment earlier. "I'm not here to take anything. I came out here to prevent *you* from taking anything."

"Me? What business is it of yours what I take?" Like a fish out of water, the body on the floor thrashed to one side then the other. The hood went flopping backward. "I'm—"

"You're a woman!"

"The owner of this cabin," she concluded.

"Mommy? Is it okay to come out of the closet now?" A tiny voice called out softly.

"And a mother!" In his mortification Jason leaped up so fast he actually went staggering backward into a wall.

In return the cabin itself punished him for his rash rudeness by raining mounted plaques of fish down on his head.

"Ow. Ooh. Ouch!" A rough-edged piece of wood bounced off his head.

He ducked the downfall the best he could, leaving his chest open for the woman's small hands to make contact and deliver a no-nonsense shove. "Who do you think you are barging into my house like that?"

"Your house? Not hardly!" He defended himself, sort of. She was so small he could hold her off by simply raising one of his hands, so that's what he did. "These cabins belong to a guy I played football with in college, Sean O'Clare. I—"

"You knew my daddy?" The closet door swung open with a bang. In a flash a kid, a girl, with long, dark hair, wearing pink jeans and an oversize garnet and black USC sweatshirt, bounded into the room.

He didn't know enough about kids to guess her age, but he did know that he was looking square at Sean O'Clare's flesh and blood. He could see it in the freckles on her pug nose, the widow's peek in her dark hair and the way her eyes lit up just to meet someone who had known her dad.

"Well, did ya? Know my dad? How? When? Can you tell me something about him?" She talked so fast he had to concentrate to distinguish the tangle of words as actual questions.

"I, uh…" Where could he begin? "I did. I knew your…dad."

Jason shook his head. He'd known Sean had married and even heard he'd started a family, but hearing about it and having it look him in the face with a look of absolute adoration and anticipation?

He kicked his way out of the pile of fish plaques, buying time to think this through. He didn't dare say the wrong thing. What did this kid with Sean's features and wearing a sweatshirt from his alma mater know about her father?

Not a whole lot, judging from the hunger in her eyes mixed with pride and awe.

It was that look that got to him, humbled him, left him at a loss for words. Finally, all he managed to say was, "It was a long time ago."

"But you did know him. You said you knew my dad." The girl came to Jason and tugged on his hand.

He'd never had a kid tug on his hand like that. He liked it, especially because it was Sean's kid.

He turned back to the kid and grinned, but not too big. "Sure, I knew your dad. We played ball together in college. He used to come to this place with me sometimes. That's how he got the idea to buy these cabins."

"*You* are Lucky Dawg Burdett?" The redhead took a step forward.

"Yeah, I reckon I am." He grinned, then dipped his head, putting his index finger to his lips, knowing full well he would look totally disarming and more than a little charming as he grinned and said, "But I like to keep the Lucky Dawg bit quiet these days."

"What? Why?" Her stance tensed. "You're from here, right? Why would you—how *could*—you keep it quiet? Doesn't it have something to do with having brothers…or wolves…"

"Brothers *or* wolves? You saying there's a difference?" Jason chuckled.

She narrowed one eye at him.

He could practically see her fitting puzzle pieces together in her mind, testing the bits and pieces of Sean's stories about Jason to see if they fit with what she saw before her now. Was he distancing himself from the name to try to trick her? To pretend he was someone he wasn't? Basically, she was trying to decide if she could trust him or not.

"Lucky Dawg." She sounded it out slowly in a very un-Southern accent that made the familiar and despised name unfamiliar and almost likable. *Luhkey D-augh-g.*

He smiled and tried to commit the pronunciation to memory.

To say she was pretty would do her a great disservice. She was not pretty. She was fresh-faced and feisty, full of what older folks in these parts would call "gumption" but not the stuff of fashion magazines or the kind of women he seemed to always end up dating, only to end up not wanting to date.

This bright-eyed woman had a boldness about her that belied her size. She couldn't have stood more than five foot three, but she had an undeniable air of substance to her—and of frailty.

Not physical frailty. She was not skinny by any means. No, she had curves. And in her approach to taking him on, he could also see that she wasn't afraid to play all angles. She was, he decided in those few seconds of sizing her up, just the right blend of fearless tomboy and intricate, amazing womanhood.

And she had been married to his oldest and dearest friend. He was looking at Sean O'Clare's widow.

He didn't know if what he had then was a light-bulb moment or perhaps a delayed reaction to taking a trout to the head, but in that moment something happened. A weight lifted. The world became brighter. The air cleared. He didn't know how to describe it, he just *knew*.

He had finally gotten what he had longed for all these years. Whether one called it an answer to his prayers or the inevitable consequence of the choices and actions put in motion just over a decade ago or both, it had happened. After all those years of coming out here to sit alone and wonder, he had finally gotten a second chance to do the right thing for Sean.

"Something about all this doesn't add up." She moved closer to the fish, which, by design or accident, put her closer to the still-open front door. "You show up here, uninvited, tackle me, tear up the place, then say you want *us* to keep quiet about *your* family nickname?"

"Actually, I'd like to keep my *family* quiet," he said. "That hasn't worked out too good for me, so far. They're one reason I came out here today."

"*One* reason?" The reticent redhead stepped now

into the shaft of light cast by the open door. "And the other reason would be?"

To pay a debt. To set everything right. To be your hero.

Each idea that popped into his head sounded hokier than the next. Finally he settled on the simple, unvarnished truth as he believed it. "I came because you're here."

Chapter Two

Because you're here? His words tripped over Charity's already raw nerves and raised gooseflesh on her skin.

What did he think? That she was some brainless bimbo who would pretend to be dazzled by some cornball line in hopes of snagging the eye of a rich…handsome…successful…man with mud in his hair.

On most men that would look just icky but this guy really pulled it off. It seemed totally natural with the faded jeans and T-shirt.

"I'm not going anywhere until I'm sure you and your daughter are safe."

"So far the only thing that has made us feel *un*safe is *you*." Except he didn't make her feel unsafe, she thought as she gazed up into those intense, amused eyes. Unsteady maybe and a little uneasy. Unnerved, yes, that was the word. The man had unnerved her with nothing more than a touch and a look. She hadn't reacted that way to anybody since…ever!

Get a grip, her inner voice demanded.

"My daughter and I are just fine. We have a lot to do here, though, so I suggest you hit the road." Charity dropped her gaze to the floor, or more accurately to the pile of plaques. Get a grip, indeed. She did, on the smallest of the pile, which she grabbed and aimed toward the open door. "And don't let the walleye hit you on the way out."

"Yeah, like you're going to throw a…"

She sent the plaque sailing out the door. She *had* come here to clear out the cabin, after all. Nobody ever said she couldn't have a little fun doing it.

"Okay, lady, I get it." He held up his hand. "I'm not welcome. You don't have to pitch a fish."

"Pitch a fish?" she repeated.

Their gazes locked.

He laughed.

What a great laugh. Husky and deep, rich and infectious.

Charity always tried to avoid infection.

She gritted her teeth. She had come here with a job to do and only a limited amount of time to do it. Every minute she wasn't working toward getting these cabins ready to sell was a minute in which her husband's family might figure out she had not gone off to the Jersey shore for a week's vacation.

Once they knew that, they'd know exactly where she *had* gone. And why she had gone.

Then they just might decide it was in Charity and her daughter's best interest to come and stop them.

She gripped another fish and gritted her teeth, fully aware of how silly she must look. Still, she threw her slender shoulders back and lifted her chin. "If I have to, I will call the authorities and have them remove you."

"You realize that I am, basically, the 'authority' sent out here in the first place, right?" He retreated along the stone fireplace, having to step carefully to move away without stepping on the glistening creatures mounted on polished wood. "So, I'm not sure what good that call would do you."

"Authority?" She could not see his face now so she didn't know if he was indulging her or setting her up for something. Charity had survived too much and come too far to be disquieted by either threat or thoughtfulness from this man. She called his bluff. "I thought you said your *family* sent you."

"In Mt. Knott that's pretty much the same thing." He kicked aside the last plaque.

Charity didn't have to see his features to know now how to motivate the man to do as she asked. "Then maybe I should call your family and tell them to call off their dog."

His back went rigid in the light from the window. "No need to get ugly, Miss, um, Mrs. O'Clare—"

"Charity. Her name is Charity." Her nine-going-on-forty-nine-year-old daughter thrust out her hand with all the push and polish of a used car sales-woman moving in to close a deal. "I'm Olivia Shawna O'Clare."

No! We're getting *rid* of him, Charity wanted to snap at her daughter. She did not want to make friends with him. Charity knew how this man treated his friends, after all. Not that that in any way dimin-ished the role of Sean's own choices and where they led him. She just didn't want her daughter getting too comfortable around this guy.

Keep your guard up, she wanted to call to her. Don't believe…

Charity couldn't complete that sentence even silently.

Everyone thought Sean had succumbed to his worst traits by dwelling too much on the stuff of dreams. But Charity knew differently. Lack of dreams, loss of hope, the perpetual mourning of those had eaten away at Sean and left an empty space he had tried to fill with everything from gambling to booze. The autopsy blamed a failure to yield for the car accident that killed him. A question of impaired judgment, the notes had read.

Impaired judgment, yes, that pretty much summed up the man she knew.

But failure to yield? They had been wrong about that. Sean had yielded too much. Her husband had given up his dreams, become discouraged and died of a discontented heart.

So Charity would not tell her bright, inquisitive, lovely and joy-filled child not to believe in the good in people, in the hope of healing, in the hand of God.

"Nice to meet you, Olivia Shawna O'Clare." Burdett met her grasp awkwardly at first, then seeming to size it all up, made allowances for the difference in the sizes of their hands. He took her fingers in his and gave them a shake. "That's an awful lot of name for someone who is, um, eight or, um—"

"Nine. I'm *nine*. Nine years, six months, two weeks and four days." She spoke in a clipped, mature tone, blissfully unaware of how that combined with the little-girl pitch of her voice made her sound achingly adorable. Well, at least to Charity.

The tall blond man probably found it all totally annoying.

She snuck a peek at the man towering over her daughter, expecting to see him smirking or rolling his eyes. She found him listening intently. So intently that it looked like he thought he might be asked to repeat the child's age later, right down to the hour and day.

Charity exhaled and relaxed her grip on the old fishing trophy she had picked up to toss out the door or use to defend her turf if the need arose.

"I'll be ten on my next birthday," Livie went on, still shaking the poor man's hand with all the subtlety.

of someone trying to prime a rusty water pump. "That's double digits, you know. Which means I'm practically a teenager."

"Even so, for someone who is practically a teenager, that is an awful lot of name," he observed. He did not shoot a knowing glance at Charity as he said this. He did not laugh. He met her child's tone and attitude with gallant enthusiasm.

Charity tried not let that sway her long-held harsh opinion of the man.

"My family calls me Livie. My friends call me Liv."

"Liv. I like that." He scratched the back of his neck then smoothed down a ruffled curl of his thick blond hair.

Charity immediately saw this as his way of wiping off the dampness from her daughter's sweaty palm without making a big deal of it. Another crack in the foundation of distrust she had built up over the years for Jason Burdett.

"Thanks!" Livie beamed up at him with an expression of pure adoration. A look Charity had not seen on her daughter's young face since Sean's death eighteen months earlier.

"My family calls me Lucky Dawg." He put his hand to his chest, almost bowing as he introduced himself. "I'd appreciate it if you'd *not* do that."

Livie nodded, her eyes wide. She hesitated a moment.

Charity braced herself, knowing the child capable of asking just about anything, from the inappropriate to the, well, major-league inappropriate.

"What did my dad call you?" Livie asked so softly and so sincerely that it seemed to suck the air out of the whole dusty old cabin.

"Jason." The man put his hand ever-so-briefly on Livie's tensed shoulder to lend comfort and reassurance as he quietly said, "Your dad called me Jason."

Jason Burdett. When Charity made up her mind to finally make the drive down from Crilley, Pennsylvania, to this property that had come to her after her husband's passing, she knew she'd have to confront some ghosts. Not of the make-believe horror movie variety, but specters of an unhappy time in her husband's life. What she had not prepared herself for was to meet one in the flesh.

He had knelt slightly in order to put himself on a more equal footing with Olivia as they spoke. Now he touched the child under the chin, then straightened up. He turned his head toward Charity and just… looked at her.

But what a look.

Her eyes met his and Charity could hardly catch her breath.

"Lucky Dawg." The name felt awkward on her tongue. She tried to repeat it the way the man had said it, all soft South Carolina drawl tinged with an amused edge of self-awareness at the ridiculousness of the whole thing. "I practically grew up hearing about you."

"Grew up?" His eyes darted for a moment to Livie and she could almost hear the keys of his mental calculator clacking. "I'm not *that* much older than you, am I?"

"Four years," Livie volunteered, holding up four fingers and managing to make herself look more like an old schoolmarm imparting a lesson than a young child butting into the adult conversation. "If you're the same age as my dad was."

"A year older, actually," Jason told the girl. "He was young in college."

"To me, he'll always be young," Charity murmured without thinking it through.

Her words seemed to strike the man like a slap in the face. He went pale. He looked at the floor.

"I knew Sean since I was younger than Livie." She pressed her back against the open door and bounced against it nervously as she told the story. "My family lived next door to his. The year Sean went to college my mom died and I moved in with his family, so I sort of…"

"Came of age hearing about me," he offered slyly.

She laughed, a little, at that and nodded. "Came of age hearing about you *and* living under the O'Clares' roof. My parents and Sean's really loved each other. They always wanted us to get married."

His head snapped up. "You got married because your families expected it?"

"No, they got married because of me!" Livie pointed her finger to her chest, proud not of the circumstances of her coming into the world, but of her maturity in knowing about them. "We don't use the *M* word."

"*M* word?" He frowned.

"Mistake." Charity was the one who felt like a kid caught with her hand in the cookie jar whenever this subject came up. "We never wanted Livie to think of herself or the relationship between her parents as a mistake."

Jason nodded.

"Motherhood and marriage made me grow up fast but it also helped me find my way back to God, to recommit my life to Christ." It had had a less profound effect on Sean but this man didn't need to know that. "Because of that I felt we had to be honest about it all. We didn't sit Livie down and spell it out for her. We just never hid the facts and when she was old enough to understand—"

"Let me guess, supersmarty here was still in diapers and came to you with a calendar and told you'd she'd done the math and wanted answers," he teased.

Livie did blush at that and giggled. Giggled!

Jason Burdett, of all people, had actually gotten through to the kid in her...well, *kid*.

No one but Sean had ever been able to do that. *Wow.* Maybe this guy wasn't the enemy. Maybe he was...

She felt her shoulders rise and fall and the air ease from her lungs in a long, wistful sigh. *A sigh?*

She gave her head a shake. None of this had gotten her anywhere.

"Anyway…" She held her hand toward the door once again. "That was more information than I needed to share and far more information that you needed to hear, Mr.…Luck…"

"Jason." Finally he extended his hand to Charity. "Sean always called me Jason, even when everybody else in the world knew me as Lucky Dawg."

She gazed into the large, open palm, but did nothing.

"Of all the people I have known in my life, Charity," he said quietly, "Sean was one of a very few who looked beyond my privileged circumstances and saw me for who I was, good and bad. No matter what transpired between him and me, I want you to know I never stopped believing in him. I never stopped praying for the best for his life."

Believing and praying. If he had said admiring and wishing, she'd have simply thanked him and sent him on his way. But a man who believed in and prayed for someone?

Charity couldn't help it; his gesture and words touched her.

Red Flag. Danger! Warning.

Charity had not come here to make friends with her husband's past. She had come to unburden herself of it.

"That's nice to know." She took the fish plaque she'd had in her left hand all this time and handed it to him. "If you'll dispose of that on your way out."

He shook his head, took the trophy and stepped onto the porch. "You really shouldn't toss these out, you know."

"I have consulted a zillion 'how to sell property fast' type articles and TV shows." She followed him onto the porch. The midmorning sun brushed the wooden steps and rocky path leading down to the lake but the overhanging roof kept them in shadow. "Never once have I seen dusty old fish listed as a big buyer turn-on."

He chuckled. Even his chuckle sounded Southern and sweet in a don't-kid-yourself, I'm-not-*that*-sweet way.

"Actually, I meant you can sell these." He smacked the plaque into his palm. "Since things have picked up around town, two of the local good ol' boys have opened up a bait shop in the old gas station a few doors down from my sister-in-law's restaurant."

"I'm listening."

"Heritage Days are coming."

"Heritage Days? Coming…here? Will they also be breaking down my front door?" she asked dryly.

He winced. "I'll fix that if you'll let me."

She waved off the offer then pointed to the fish and made a hurry-it-along motion for him to get him talking about selling them again.

"During the opening weekend of Heritage Days the county holds a fishing tournament on Bass Lake."

"I'm still listening, but beginning to lose interest." She put her hand on her hip.

He leaned his raised forearm against one of the columns that supported the porch's roof. "These are trophies from past tournaments. The new store is one of the sponsors. They'd love to get their hands on some of these to display. Just take a few in and tell Jed and Warren that…I sent you."

"You mean Lucky Dawg?"

He cringed this time, paused, then nodded.

His open distaste for but good-natured tolerance of that name only added to his charm. Which only added to Charity's desire to get him gone. She had not come to Carolina to soak up charm, no matter how interestingly it was packaged. "Come back for the open house if you like. I plan to have this place on the market in less than two weeks."

"If you can, see someone right away and get the sign up before Heritage Days. More people come into town for that than you might imagine."

"Thanks," she said. "Nice meeting you at last."

"Yeah. You, too," he said softly, then, lifting his head, called into the cabin. "You, too, Liv. Really great meeting you."

"You're not going, are you?" Liv appeared in the doorway, her eyes wide. "What about that intruder you were yelling about?"

Livie darted out onto the porch and snatched at the man's large hand. Once she nabbed it, she dug her heels in and leaned back like a fisherman trying to reel in a prize catch. "You scared Mom so bad she dropped her cell phone and made me hide in the closet. Now suddenly nobody cares about that?"

"Livie, honey, *we're* the intruders." Charity set the mounted fish on a bench piled high with random junk just outside the cabin's front door. "We're not in any danger out here. It was all a simple misunderstanding."

"Yeah." Jason gave the kid a knowing nod in support of her mother's assessment. "Y'all really should have let people know you were working out here these past two weeks."

"Two weeks?" A chill shimmied down Charity's spine.

"We don't get much excitement around here," he went on. "Something as compelling as an unfamiliar face or, as one round of gossip put it, an 'unsettling presence' out at Twin Cabins Lake is bound to get the locals all stirred up."

"An unsettling…" Charity pulled Livie close.

"No way!" Livie piped up. "Two weeks ago I was still in school. It let out three days ago. We just got here this morning!"

"Then it wasn't you those other times?" Jason's expression grew dark and wary.

Charity hugged Livie closer still, so close the child actually began to wriggle to get free.

"Probably just a kid." Jason tried to sound reassuring without actually reassuring her at all.

"But if it's not?" She wanted to know. She *had* to know.

"Maybe you shouldn't be out here alone until we're sure."

Charity held her breath and considered that. She had come here to find her independence. To show Livie that a person could make his or her dreams come true if they didn't depend on dreams alone. Faith and hard work and good choices—she had come here to teach her child these cornerstones for a good life.

The minute she had heard him speak his name, she had thought of Jason Burdett as the last person on earth to help her do those things. Fat lot of help he'd been to Sean in those areas. And now…

"I guess it would be all right if you stuck around," she heard herself say. "Just while we clean up today and I figure out what to do. We'll stay at the hotel on the highway tonight so it won't interfere with your…" She pressed her lips together, not sure how to put this delicately. "Um, evening plans."

"I don't have any evening plans," he said, lowering his arm from the column and taking a step back toward the door. "And I'd be happy to help you out on one condition."

Charity tensed. "What's that?"

He bent down and scooped up the walleye from the porch floor where she had whizzed it past his head earlier and made a swing with it as though employing some strange Southern martial art move. "No more fish of fury."

Livie giggled again.

Charity sighed. "I can't promise you anything, not if you keep making awful jokes like that one."

"Fine." He tossed the walleye onto the bench by the other fish then stuck his hand out to her. "No more fishy wordplays, no more playing fishy Frisbee. Truce?"

Charity looked at his open hand again. A hand that probably shook Sean's a thousand times but when he needed it, was withdrawn. She looked at the cabin across the lake, then at the porch around her, then at Livie.

She grasped his hand, trying not to think about how warm it felt, how strong or how safe her own small fingers felt enveloped in his large hand. She'd take his help only long enough to find her own solution.

"Truce."

Her course was set, for now, but courses, like dreams and plans, change. She would not put too much stock in this one.

Chapter Three

"Ugh!" Charity dropped her end of the long green-and-silver canoe on the shore and brushed her hands along the sides of her jeans. "Is everything out here covered in grimc?"

"Not everything." Jason pushed up the sleeves of the flannel shirt he'd found in one of the closets. He hadn't counted on the coolness created by the shade of pines and the breeze off the lake even in late May so he'd thrown it on. When he drew his hand away, he looked at the gray film on his hand. "Some things are, however, covered in cobwebs."

"Cobwebs!" She jumped and shook and brushed at her clothes, saying, "It's like I can still feel them all over me."

"And we still have one more cabin to go," he reminded her, jerking his thumb over his shoulder toward the intended destination.

She looked up at him. One long, graceful curve of red hair clung to her flushed cheek. "Why am I doing this again?"

"From where I am standing…" Jason, still holding his end of the canoe—and of the bargain to stick around all day—up, cocked his head.

He dropped his gaze to his ridiculously expensive shoes sinking into the mud along the shore of the lake, then at the petite woman a few feet away. Even just standing there, huffing from struggling with her part of the canoe, puffing a strand of hair out of her eyes or flicking a leaf off her sweatshirt sleeve, she had an effect on him.

He'd fought it all morning as they had gone about the preliminaries of going over the first cabin. While they pried open windows too-long closed and shone lights into places too-long dark, he had watched her.

He learned a lot about Charity from seeing her interact with Liv. He'd heard it said once that you never really knew how much you could care about a woman until you saw how much she loved your children. He had never understood that until today.

Of course, Liv wasn't his daughter and Charity wasn't his wife, but watching them brought out feelings in him that he had never even suspected himself capable of. And they reminded him that all the blessings and success in the world didn't mean much if a man didn't mean something to people who loved and counted on him.

"From where I'm standing, you aren't actually doing anything." It came out like a good-natured jab at her but as soon as the words left his mouth he couldn't help turning them back on himself. All these years he had prayed for and even pitied Sean, but look what that man had!

Charity and Olivia.

Weighing his cars and reputation and even his work against that, Jason was the one who felt he hadn't actually done anything. Nothing big, nothing important, nothing lasting, at least.

He lowered his side of the canoe slowly until just the end of it rested afloat in the water.

"C'mon, Mom, I want to get to the other side and explore that cabin!" Liv churned her arm in the air, beckoning her mother to get moving.

"You want to get there so quick, take that little path where we left the SUV." Charity pointed up a small incline just north of the main cabin to the battered wooden sign that marked the entrance to Camp Store Cabin Trail.

Liv did a double take. "Can I? Really?"

"Go ahead. We should be able to see you the whole way." Charity's fingers sank into the thick fabric of her sweatshirt at her neck, then flexed and massaged their way down to her shoulder. She dropped her head forward, seemingly to get to some hard-to-reach aching muscle, but clearly she wanted to keep her daughter from knowing she had had second thoughts about her own idea as she muttered under her breath to him, "That's safe for her, right?"

He smiled at both her desire to give her child a sense of independence and her inability to entirely let the kid strike out on her own just yet.

"It's a long walk," he said quietly. "But if you grab the supplies and hop in the canoe right now and start rowing, we should get there way ahead of her."

"Do we have to hop?" she asked even as she aimed the toe of her hiking boot at the tip of the canoe and nudged it toward the water.

The end nearest him dipped and buoyed. In response Jason did hop, though not into the canoe but away from it.

Glug.

Slosh.

He lifted his leg and shook his head at the droplets of water on his jeans, socks and shoes. "Get in and let's go."

She took one look at the seat he had indicated, the one nearest to him. She sniffed then swooped down to collect the canvas bag that they had filled with flashlights, cleaning supplies and tools and promptly plunked herself down on the side still onshore.

"You need to be on this side so I can shove us off," he told her.

"No, thanks." She crinkled up her nose. "I get motion sickness if I ride backward."

"You get motion sickness?" He folded his arms and narrowed his eyes. "In a canoe?"

"I don't know." She pushed the bag off her lap. "But why chance it?"

When it dropped into the belly of the old canoe with a remarkably loud thud, Jason took a peek beneath the craft. It had snagged on a rock that could act as an impediment or a pivot that could slide them off course or dump them out if they didn't free themselves of it before trying launch.

He grinned. "You like getting your own way, don't you?"

"I like making my own decisions," she said slowly.

"Same difference."

"Not exactly. This is my choice." She pointed to the seat beneath her. "I plan to take charge of every aspect of my life from now on, even in the small things."

"Then you'd better get used to disappointment." He gave the end nearest him a push with his foot and sent the long craft spinning.

"Who-o-oa!"

Another quick action with his foot and she came to a stop with her back to the lake.

She put her fists on her hips and glared at him. "I can't believe you did that!"

"Pretty slick, huh?" He laughed. "Hope you learned a lesson from that."

"Aside from the fact that it's not really your place to try to teach *me* lessons…" she closed her eyes and took a deep breath, then opened them again and concluded, "...I guess I did learn that I am not the only one who likes having things their own way."

She'd pretty much missed the point all around but she was just so appealing doing it, he couldn't help but shake his head and enjoy the moment. "Well, I was going to say something about needing to have all the facts before you make up your mind. Maybe toss in a little reminder that everybody needs a little help making the right decisions from time to time, but it's really not my place to try to teach *you* anything."

"I'm not saying... I hope I didn't sound..."

"Yeah. I get it." If he was going to enjoy the moment, he might as well *really* enjoy it. "Don't waste your breath telling me how right I am."

"Right? Waste my breath? I'd rather hold it until I turn blue."

"Save that until we're across the lake, will ya?" He took a second to decide how best to proceed launching the canoe into the lake. "Right now you need all the lung power you can muster. Grab that oar."

She opened her mouth.

He held one finger up. "Conserve air by not arguing and when I tell you to, use your oar to push off from the shallow water."

"What are *you* going to be doing?" she asked with the faintest residue of resentment in her tone as she obeyed his directive.

He pushed her end of the canoe partially into the lake. It dipped then rolled slightly then settled. "Keeping tabs on the status of your lunch. How ya feeling? Stomach okay?"

She hesitated a moment then seemed to realize that he was trying to get them moving and she wasn't helping. She nodded and gave him a big thumbs-up.

"Great!" He slipped off his shoes and socks and lobbed them into the canoe.

He bent and began rolling up his jeans. When he caught Charity studying him curiously, he held out his hands to present himself in his borrowed cobweb-covered shirt with his legs exposed from the knees down. "How about now? Starting to feel a little queasy yet?"

Her raised thumb wavered slightly.

He laughed.

So did she.

"Mom! Look where I am!" Liv waved to them from a high spot near the beginning of the path. "Race ya!"

"No running," Charity called out. As soon as the girl waved and started off again, the young mother fixed her brown eyes with a gleam of mischief in them on him and said, "Get a move on. When she gets on the other side we should be sitting there with our heads down pretending we'd waited so long for her we've fallen asleep from boredom."

"Boredom?" In her company? Impossible. He waded in and guided the canoe until he could climb in and sit down. "Okay, let's get started then. Now comes the fun part."

"Riding backward?" She did look a little green.

"No, working as a team."

He picked up his oar and used it to propel them out of the shallows while she watched intently.

Too intently.

He cleared his throat.

She leaned forward, stretching her upper body over the oar resting in her lap.

He fixed his gaze on hers. A bead of sweat trickled down the back of his neck. He sank his oar in the water and used all his strength for one smooth, long stroke. It sent them into the lake proper and when he lifted the oar from the water, the canoe bobbled slightly.

That made her sit up. She took her eyes off him to glance around.

Seizing the moment, Jason slipped off the flannel shirt. Not because he had any vain notion of giving her a better view of him being all outdoorsy and muscular in his old Just Another Crumb from Carolina snack cake factory tour T-shirt and dorky rolled-up jeans. But it had dawned on him that this whole team concept might be asking too much of the fiercely independent redhead. If he had to paddle them the whole distance, he didn't need a borrowed shirt restricting his range of motion.

Deftly, he pulled the oar out of the water, swung

it over to the other side of the canoe and plunged it into the seemingly placid surface of the lake again.

"Hurry up, slowpokes!" Liv hollered at them from a point about a quarter of the way around.

"I'm doing my part." He twisted his head and shoulder toward the kid but kept watch on Charity from the corners of his eyes as he yelled, "But your mom can't seem to get her oar in the water."

"C'mon, Mom! If you want to get anywhere, you've got to paddle your own canoe." Liv pantomimed the proper motion.

Charity frowned at her.

"I think your daughter has a future writing inspirational slogans for those motivational posters." He kept paddling, moving them closer to the center of the narrow finger lake.

"I'm perfectly capable of getting myself across this lake," she called to her child, who had already forged onward.

Forging onward, what an apt description of both of these O'Clare females.

"I was just watching you to try to figure out what to do." Charity aimed her attention and abundant energy his way.

"Gotcha. Here's the proper hold." He showed her the oar then took one hand off and moved his index finger in a circle. "And the proper way to—"

Her hand shot up in the universal sign for "stop right there, pal" or sometimes "stop in the name of love."

This time, judging from her pale, thin lips and the fire in her eyes, it was definitely a *pal* situation. "You do not have to tell me what to do like I'm some incompetent child."

Even though he knew that wasn't really aimed at him but at everyone who had trampled on her need for self-determination before him, he couldn't just sit there and say nothing. He made the gesture with his finger again. "All right. But—"

Again with the hand. "I came here to find my way out of a life where people have always tried to tell me what to do."

"I totally get that. But you—"

"I will figure this out."

He eased out a big breath, put the paddle in the water again and moved them closer to their goal.

"You said we'd work as a team," she said, her sincere eyes accentuating her single-minded nature. "That comes with certain expectations, you know."

"Hey, you don't have to tell me about expectations. I've spent my whole life tiptoeing around them. I'm an expert at it," he muttered as he made another long, even stroke with the oar.

"Then you should know that in no way does my agreeing to work as a team imply that you get to play the Big Cheese while relegating me to the role of…of…"

"Cheese doodle?" He had to say it. He just *had* to.

"What did you call me?"

Water lapped at the side of the canoe.

Jason gave an offhanded shrug. "You spend your whole life tiptoeing around other people's expectations, one day, you just gotta put your foot down."

"Are you saying you think you *are* the Big Cheese?"

"I'm saying I thought we were going with a sort of fromage there." He overplayed it with the snooty attitude because it seemed more fun than simply telling her to lighten up. "So I went with it. Big cheese? Cheese doodle?"

He switched his oar again, more paddling.

A lost look from those deep, vulnerable brown eyes.

The canoe went gliding past the center of the lake.

"You think you can use humor to keep me in my place?" Her shoulders went back. Her bright curly hair practically bristled.

He wanted to ask her who had hurt her this badly. Who had pushed her into corners so often that she had become this frightened and defensive over such a small remark? But he thought he knew the answer to that.

Sean O'Clare came from a dominating family that liked to tell people what to do. Sean's life had gone terribly and tragically awry despite their efforts. Who would they blame? Who would they push into the corner?

He had seen her all day as Sean's widow. As Liv's mom. As someone he wished he could know better.

Well, he'd just gotten his wish and it made his heart ache for her.

One mighty stroke and they had gained enough distance that they would easily reach the other side before Liv. "I wasn't trying to teach you anything."

"Okay then." At last she took her oar from her lap and after a couple of tries successfully mimicked the proper positions of her hands on the oar handle. "Okay. I didn't meant to overreact. This has been difficult and emotional and it's just the first day, you know?"

He nodded. "You know what else I know?"

"What?" She stuck the end of the oar out of the canoe at last but it didn't actually touch the water.

"If I ever want to get you really *cheesed off,* all I have to do is give you an order." Another stroke, a deep one this time, to test the depths of the water. Not much farther now. "And call you a doodle."

"That's not funny." She closed her lips tight and fixed a squinty-eyed glare at him but she couldn't maintain the ferocious and detached act.

A small snort. She reined it in.

"Then don't laugh," he ordered as he pulled his oar from the water entirely.

A barely contained sputter that she tried to disguise with a cough.

He leaned forward, never taking his eyes from her quickly reddening face and whispered, "Doodle."

That did it.

She busted out laughing.

He joined her. It felt good to share just a few moments with her free of guilt, anxiety or stuffed fish.

With the tension eased, he decided she might just listen to directions now. "Look, if we plan on taking the canoe back and have to work together for that, what you need to do—"

"I know, I know." She stuck her oar in the water, gritted her teeth and, as she gave a stroke that sent them slightly back in the direction they had just come from, said proudly, "I have to paddle my own canoe."

"No," he said in a deep, still voice as he reached out and pried the paddle from her hands to keep her from doing that again. "You have to find it in your heart to trust that there are some people who actually want to help you reach your goals."

He dipped his head then to indicate the second cabin just up the small slope that led to the lake where they had just almost come aground.

She turned around and gasped. "We're here."

"Yep." He got out. His feet hit the water and when they sank in ankle deep his toes touched the rocky shore. He sucked in his breath at the jolt of cold then moved alongside the canoe to drag it up on the shore.

"I talked the whole way about doing things for myself while you did all the work for me." She shook her head, clearly embarrassed.

"Look at it this way." He flipped the tow rope

over a stump. "Kept you from thinking about your motion sickness."

"I feel pretty awful now anyway." She sighed, her hands in her lap.

Liv appeared in the clearing, waving her arms and jumping. "I made it! Here I am! Did you see me? I did it all by myself."

"We don't have to tell Liv if you don't want to," he said as he got his shoes and the canvas bag and chucked them onto dry land.

She shook her head. "I don't lie to her and I don't keep secrets from her."

"Good policy," he agreed, stretching out his arm to offer her something steady to lean on as she got out. "But you'd better be careful. The kid might accidentally learn a few things that way."

She looked at his open hand then at her approaching daughter. Finally she settled her fingers in his and started to step out.

The canoe rocked.

She lurched forward.

He bent to catch her.

She got her footing then looked into his eyes, just inches from hers.

If she had been any other girl at any other time, he just might have kissed her. Might? He lost himself in those deep brown eyes. He definitely would have kissed her.

He couldn't imagine that she'd welcome a kiss

from him, from the man who had let her husband down and put him on the path that resulted in his own destruction. What could she ever feel for him?

"Jason?" she murmured.

"Hmm?"

"I can stand on my own, you know."

"Oh. Yeah." He stepped away but in his reluctance to let her go so soon, knowing he might never hold her this close again, let his hand slide along her arm.

"For the record," she whispered as she grabbed his hand seconds before he would have lost touch. "I'm not opposed to learning things. I just don't like people thinking I need to be taught a lesson. Does that make sense?"

It did. A lot of sense. He gave her hand a squeeze. "It's a matter of attitude."

"Yes. And respect. And…"

"Trust," he echoed his earlier thought.

"I suppose so. Yes. Trust," she murmured.

"Good to know." He straightened and finished helping her onto the slope where Liv waited excitedly.

She took a few steps away from him.

He hated the very thought of her not trusting him, of her moving onward—if onward meant away from him. In that second, he made up his mind.

Walking behind her up to the cabin, he bent to speak directly into her ear. "Since you don't mind learning a few things from someone you trust, then

I guess you won't mind learning one really important thing from me?"

"What?" She slowed her pace.

He matched it as he smiled with his lips so close to her ear her hair moved with the breath it took to say, "Whether you are paddling your own canoe or part of a team, if you really want to get someplace? You ought to be facing the direction you are going."

As the realization of her backward stance in the canoe hit her, she gasped like she'd just had an ice cube down her back.

"Otherwise, even when you arrive, you might not know if that's really where you want to be." With that he strode on past her, determined to get to the cabin ahead of her and her daughter. "And whether you like it or not, for the time being, you and I are going the same direction."

Chapter Four

"I would have figured it out on my own," she called to the man taking long, confident strides up to the cabin that mirrored the one they had worked in most of the day. She would have. "Eventually."

If she stuck around long enough.

...for the time being, you and I are going the same direction.

Charity shivered. Probably a cool spring breeze off the lake, she told herself. She didn't lie to Livie but that didn't mean that sometimes she didn't play a little hide-and-seek with the truth from herself. Jason Burdett got to her.

There were a hundred reasons, maybe a thousand, why she shouldn't allow that to happen. Only right now, watching him all strong and capable, take charge and unafraid of acting corny... She sighed.

A thousand reasons. And she couldn't think of a one.

She took off after him. "I would have figured it out and done the right thing."

"Figured out what, Mom?" Liv had to skip, lope, take a few running steps then skip again, just to keep up with Charity hustling to keep up with Jason.

"Y'all hang back a second. I want to scope this place out, just in case."

Charity nabbed the girl around the shoulders and held her back.

"Figure what out?" Liv asked again.

Charity watched him fish a flashlight from the bag then reposition his hand on the skinny part of the oar he had to take a defensive one-hand grip.

"Figure out how to paddle my own canoe," she whispered into Liv's hair, suddenly wondering if they should retreat to that canoe.

"Oh, Mom, that's silly. Paddle a canoe? You've seen people do it on TV." Liv slipped from her mother's arms to demonstrate the same motion Jason had used to get them here. "Just point yourself in the direction you want to go and, you know…"

Even her nine-year-old knew what to do.

"But sometimes on TV the people in a canoe face each other," Charity protested.

"Aw, only in mushy old movies when the lady is all girly and makes goofy eyes at the boy and likes to carry around an umbrella." She held her hands up, clutching an imaginary handle and batting her eyelashes so much as she walked around playacting that she made herself stagger slightly.

"That's not an umbrella. It's called a parasol."

"Is that what you wanted, Mom?" Liv stood still. She cocked her head, her tone decidedly suspicious. "To float around on the lake looking at Mr. Lucky Dawg and twirling a parasail?"

"Para*sol*. A parasail is like…like a big kite you ride on behind a boat flying through the air."

"Is that what you want, Mom?" Livie didn't miss a beat jumping back into the same question she'd asked before, only with a few nine-year-old giggling-girl improvements. "To fly around up in the air because you're so in lo-o-ove?"

"Livie!" She glanced toward Jason, who had reached the path just a few feet from the cabin's front steps.

Livie put her hands over her mouth and giggled.

"I didn't… I *don't*… You shouldn't go around saying things like that. People will get the wrong idea."

"What idea is that?" Jason had come back to where they stood in the grass.

"Mom wants to fly around with an umbrella and make her eyes go like this…" Her eyelashes fluttered again and she affected a huge high-pitched sigh, her hands clasped under her chin.

"Enough," Charity warned her child, though not harshly, because she figured she deserved a little ribbing for the distracted way she had acted. Determined to dispense with that kind of thing from now on, she started up the hill. "So, let's get to work."

Jason held out his arm to stop her, his hand stretched out flat shoulder level in front of her. "Plenty for you and the kid to do down here by the canoe. Why don't you look for, uh…make sure the, um…did I tell you about Ol' Turkey?"

"There's a turkey running around out here?" Charity frowned at him, then dipped her gaze to his hand.

"It's not a turkey. It's a fish named Ol' Turkey. Big fish." He spread his hands out to show the size. "He's like a legend around here."

"Wow." Livie held her own hands out. Matching her fingertips to Jason's, she held them up for Charity to see. "That's huge."

"Yeah." Jason squatted to put himself on Livie's level. As he spoke he stretched his arm out toward the lake to help paint the picture. "Every year dozens of people report they see him, some swear they got a hook in him, but so far no one has succeeded in landing him."

"Why don't you two wade out and try to grab him grizzly bear style?" Charity threw her hands up and turned on her heel. "I'm heading up to the cabin."

"Wouldn't you rather stay here and look for Ol' Turkey?" Jason hurried uphill to cut her off. "You and Livie. Close to the canoe? In case you see…uh…Ol' Turkey and want to…*need* to…"

"He's not done looking for the sneaky guy, Mom."

Livie looked up at Charity, her expression back to the serious, smart girl Charity recognized so readily. "He wants us to stay by the canoe so we can get away if he finds him."

"I was trying not to say that to keep from scaring you, kid." Jason shook his head and looked Charity straight in the eye. "I want to go inside the cabin to look for signs of that sneaky guy, not to mention signs of, let's say, intelligent-*ish* life?"

"Looking for *intelligent-ish* life? If I were a person who hadn't just come across the lake backward, I'd be tempted to warn you not to look in any mirrors," Charity teased.

"He means like mice and snakes and stuff, Mom." Liv shook her head.

"Mice and...snakes?" She hadn't even thought about that. "You mean there could have been mice and snakes in the other cabin and I just went barging in?"

Jason bent down to speak directly to Livie. "You keep your mom here." He pointed to the ground. "While I go make sure there are no signs of any of that inside the second cabin."

"Yes, sir." She gave a snappy salute.

"Now, if you'll just give me the key, I'll get this over with." He held his hand out to Charity.

"Oh, sure." Mice and snakes and sneaky guys inside her cabin. She hadn't thought about that. She slipped her hand into the pocket of her sweatshirt, suddenly glad for his offer to go in first. "I've got it right here. The...key."

"Metal thing. About this big?" He held his thumb and forefinger the proper distance apart.

"Yes, yes." She searched her jeans pockets. "I thought for sure I'd put it in here." She gave her sweatshirt pocket a shake.

"Maybe it fell out when you did the dance of disgust."

"The what?"

His body stiffened and he wagged his head around and he made girly squeals. Each time he added a new twist to his imitation, Livie laughed harder.

"What?" Charity dug her fingers into the corners of the stretchy fabric and found only lint. "When did I ever do that?"

"Does the mention of cobwebs ring a bell?" he prodded.

"Ooh." She shuddered at the thought, remembered her reaction to thinking about having them all over her, then gazed across the way.

The stuck SUV. The dingy cabins. The stuffed fish. Mice and snakes. The wrong-way-round canoe ride. The impossible man. Now the missing keys.

When she had driven here this morning, she had known exactly what she wanted in her life and it didn't include a single one of those things. Now? She wasn't so sure about at least one of them.

Oh, and she really wished she had those keys.

She pressed her fingers to her temples and shut her eyes. "This has been such a long day."

Jason put his hand firmly on Livie's shoulder. "From now on you are in charge of canoe paddling *and* keys."

"Maybe we should just go back to the other side and deal with this tomorrow?" No matter how much she pushed and rubbed, the dull throb would not ease in her head. She'd spent too many hours out here today accomplishing nothing. She needed a good night's sleep to give her some perspective. "I still have to get my SUV unstuck."

"I already asked the guy who takes care of the delivery trucks at my family's factory to come by and take care of it." He narrowed his eyes and gazed at the other side of the lake in the general direction of the place where she had left her SUV. "Should be okay when we're done here."

"Wow." She looked across the lake, too. If Jason hadn't shown up when he did, her already long day might have gone on indefinitely. "Thanks."

He grinned, more shyly than cocky. "It's what I do."

She felt her own mouth curve upward in response to his humble heroics. "Take care of people?"

He looked surprised. As if no one had ever said that about him before. "I, uh, I always thought of it as taking care of business."

Business. How could she have forgotten that? Jason Burdett was first and foremost a man of business. If it did not profit him, he did not bother with it. He had been sent out here by his family and checking out the whole place was part of that duty. She wouldn't be rid of him and able to get on to her own business until he did.

"Okay. We're here now. Let's not stretch this out over another day." She started up the hill. "Livie, stay out of the water but close to the canoe. This won't take a minute and if it's all right, we'll come back or call for you."

"We?" He trailed only for a few steps before he overtook her. "I understand the whole wanting to do for yourself, Charity, but this isn't an affront to your self-reliance. This is common sense and safety."

"We've been out here all day and nothing has happened. Nor have we happened upon so much as a sign of anything that has happened in the past." Her legs strained to take the steepest part of the rise just before it leveled out to the lot with the cabin on it. She had to take a break, but rather not let Jason see how drained this stressful day had left her. She used the break to take in the view from this new vantage point.

Twin Cabins Lake was gorgeous. The water, though not crystal clear, had a glasslike perfection when looked at over a distance. Yet the steady, gentle lap of waves suggested an unseen undercurrent. What a perfect analogy for her feelings this day.

On the shore Livie looked so small, not because she was so far away but because her surroundings seemed so vast. Endless almost, though Charity knew the exact number of acres of the property that had come to her after Sean's death.

She drew in the clean, earth-and-lake-scented air and hugged her arms around her body. The tall pines that framed it formed a still and protective shelter from the outside world. If only they really could do that. Safeguard Livie and her from...

She lifted her eyes to Jason.

Charity feared so many things. Losing herself, losing her independence, losing her best hopes for Livie to feel strong and able to follow her dreams. In breaking away from the O'Clares she had taken the first step toward overcoming those fears, making them a distant memory. She would not jeopardize that bold move now by giving this place and the man so closely associated with it the power to alter her plans, even slightly.

"I plan to come out here several more times before I stick a For Sale sign in the front. I refuse to live in fear of a rumor of an 'unsettling presence.'" Her head hurt. Her muscles quivered from fatigue. Still, she could not rest, not yet.

She started up again and when she hit the level lot, marched right up to the steps. "Even without the key we can do a quick go-round of the cabin, peek in the windows, check for signs of forced entry."

"Thanks to me, we know what that looks like." Jason reached her side in only a few long strides. "But on the bright side, if we really want in, we already know I can break the door down."

"Please don't. I have enough issues with the way we left the door at the other cabin." The throbbing behind her eyes grew more intense as the image of the door "bolted" tight with a spare oar wedged in the door frame by Jason, who then climbed out a window.

"Hey, my patented oar-in-the-door method is practically foolproof."

She put her hands on her hips and studied the second log cabin with its drab green shutters and roof, broad, cluttered porch and stash of old metal signs leaning against the railings. It was clearly not good for much of anything, but weekend getaways by people content to spend their time just a half step up from camping in a tent. And they expected to pay accordingly. It was not a home. It was not even a home-away-from-home.

"The trouble is that *only* a fool would want to break into a place like this," she said.

And what did that say about a person who would want to *buy* it? That realization hit Charity coming and going. What did her snap judgment about this place say about Sean? What did it say about Jason's choice not to become his partner in this mess? And most of all, what did it say about the possibility of a quick sale to fund her new life before the O'Clares intervened?

"Well, you know what they say about fools rushing in." He held out his hand to offer his service in breaking down the door. "Shall we?"

Fools rush in but she was no fool. She might be trying with every ounce of faith and love and hope left in her to give Livie the power to follow her dreams, but in order to do that, Charity knew she had to always stay on her guard. Face the direction she was headed. That meant not getting distracted by anything—or anyone.

"Let's get this done so I can move on to the next phase."

Chapter Five

"Maybe I've been too hasty." Charity sat up in bed in the dim hotel room. She pushed back the almost sumptuous layering of crisp sheet, cotton blanket and authentic Carolina handcrafted quilt.

Livie, who had come on this trip with an expectation of camping out, crawled out of the sleeping bag that she had insisted on using on the floor beside the large bed. "What's hasty? And how are you too much of it?"

"Hasty means hurried basically, but in this case it means too quick to make up my mind." She could hardly believe her own words. She shifted just slightly and every muscle from her neck to her toes twinged. She sucked air between her teeth.

"Make up your mind about what?"

Jason Burdett.

"Accepting help with all the lake cabin projects."

Charity chose her words carefully. "I wonder now if I can really do it all by myself."

"I'll help!" Livie thrashed her legs and kicked the last of her sleeping bag off her bare feet. She sprang up and threw her hands high in the air, jumping up in a way that made her long, dark braid bounce. "I'll help, Mom. I'll help."

"You betcha you'll help!" Charity reaffirmed her child's importance. "But even with you pitching in, when I think of the list of chores we have after checking out both cabins…"

Livie sank down to sit atop her crumpled sleeping bag again. She scrunched her face up and rubbed her hands together, switching gears to play the part of the brains behind the operation. "We need some serious muscle."

"I've got serious muscle aches." Charity pressed her fingertips into her stiff neck. "Do they count?"

"Duh, Mom. That's why we need—"

"A good night's sleep every night. It has done wonders for me already." Charity cut her daughter off. She did not want to have a conversation with Livie about Jason first thing in the morning. "All this clean, fresh air really improved my rest."

"Fresh air?" Livie took a big sniff then wrinkled up her nose. "It must be better up there than down here."

"I didn't mean in the hotel, I meant…all around." Charity gave a one-shouldered shrug. Even that slight movement made her wince. "They say it makes you sleep better."

Though she could not discount the sweet dreams of living in a cabin on a lake surrounded by pines and spending her days in the company of a certain tall blond man.

Keep your guard up. Stay on course.

The longer she stayed in the Mt. Knott area, Charity now realized, the easier she'd find it to stray from her plans. For so long now trying to save Sean, trying to please his family, trying to give Livie the best care and guidance had totally engulfed her. Now, she suspected that paddling her own canoe might not come as easily as she hoped. Thoughts of Jason Burdett only made that suspicion worse.

She clutched the collar of her pajama top and eased her breath out slowly. "I was just trying to decide if the fresh air or the hard work had more to do with my sleeping so well."

"Why?"

"Well, if it was the work, I'd know I have to keep slogging away at it." She tipped back her head, stuck out her tongue and threw her arm up to lay her wrist over her brow, hoping to get a laugh or at least a smidgen of pity.

"Ugh, that's awful." Livie mimicked her mother, only instead of just tipping her head back, she flopped backward onto her pillow as though totally done in by the very thought of all that effort.

Charity sat up and clapped softly, pleased with her daughter's amateur dramatics. "If, on the other hand, it's the fresh air, well, then all we have to do for the rest of our stay is breathe."

"And make Mr. Lucky Dawg do all the work!" Livie clapped her hands, too, at the thought.

Charity's hands sank to her lap. "I can't promise we'll see Jason Burdett again during our stay here, sweetie."

"Why?"

Because he scares me. Because I thought I had everything all figured out until I spent time with him. I thought that Jason and your grandparents were the bad guys in your dad's life and I needed to distance myself from them to keep you from suffering your dad's fate. Now I don't know if I believe that anymore, at least about Jason, but even if there is a chance that that's true...

She had to stay on course.

"Jason is a busy man, a *businessman,* and our cabins and what we do with our time is simply not any of his business."

"But I liked him. I'd *like* to see him again. I never did get him to tell me much about Daddy."

He's hardly the one to ask! Charity reined in her gut response to her child wanting to hear about her father from a practical stranger. "If you want to know about Daddy, you can always ask me."

The child's quiet gaze fell to the floor. She

smoothed down her sleeping bag. "I don't want to make you sad."

"Oh, sweetie." Tears crowded into the corners of her eyes and collected along her bottom lashes. She wanted to swoop down on her precious little girl and hug her close but knew that seeing her tears and emotional outburst would close Livie off again.

That was the kind of thing the O'Clares might do. Weeping and hugging were big with the O'Clares. She certainly understood their pain. She just couldn't remain the focal point of it any longer. She had to break free and she had to give Livie that same opportunity. She had to tell the truth, to stop looking back because they were not headed in that direction.

Charity set her shoulders straight and reached deep within herself to find a tentative smile. "I know I was cranky yesterday and might have made it seem like I didn't want you to talk about him, but don't ever hold back talking about your father because of that."

"But I just thought—"

"I miss him, yes." *Be honest. Reassure her.* "And sometimes when I think about what might have been, I *am* sad, but that's okay. *I'm* okay."

She perked up. "You do sound happier this morning."

"Than I sounded yesterday?"

"And the day before that and the day before that and the day before…"

"Oh, Livie." She could not stop the tears from

rolling down her cheek then. She wiped them away with the back of her hand and did not let her child retreat, but opened up her arms to invite her in. "Have I been so very hard to live with?"

Livie jumped up from the floor. She crawled into the bed with Charity, the way she often had in those first weeks after Sean died, and snuggled close. "No, Mom. I like living with you. Not that I minded living with Grandie and Grandpop, but I like it being just us again."

"Me, too." Charity pushed aside her own red curls smooshed against her cheek in order to kiss the child's warm head. She sniffled, the tears subsiding as she lost herself in the closeness of her daughter and the child-like smell of her strawberry shampoo. "I know this past year, moving in with your grandparents to help save money, wasn't ideal, but look where it's gotten us."

"Yeah, this is just the best hotel ever, isn't it?" Her eyes lit up.

Charity took a sweeping visual tour of the dimly lit room with the painted white furniture, aqua carpet, striped green and white vinyl wallpaper and gold-framed still life of fruit bolted to the wall. She put her nose to Livie's, rubbed it and laughed. "Not the hotel, sweetie. I mean here in Mt. Knott."

"Oh, Mt. Knott is even better!" She pulled away as though she had to create more space to contain all her enthusiasm, which bubbled up and out of her like a fountain. "I love the cabins. And the lake. And the canoe. It's just about perfect here."

Just about. But not quite.

"You only feel that way because it's new and fun. Once you'd been around a while don't you think you'd get bored living in a small town?"

"Is that why Dad didn't ever come down here?" Livie climbed out of the bed and began gathering up her pillow and sleeping bag. "He got bored with it?"

Charity drew in her breath. She'd told her daughter they could talk about Sean. "I wouldn't say bored, exactly."

Angered over the loss of his chance at playing football professionally? Betrayed by Jason in their would-be business partnership? Frustrated with his efforts to please his family? Embarrassed by the improbability of making this place viable? In denial about his own role in it all?

She wanted to tell the truth to her child, but how did you tell a kid the truth when she wasn't old enough to understand it? When, no matter how many times you went over it yourself, there were so many things you couldn't understand?

"Jason had brought your dad to Mt. Knott when they were in college, and your dad loved it here. He thought of Jason like a brother."

"He thought of Jason like Uncle Davey?"

"No, not exactly like Uncle Davey." Charity shook her head at the thought of Sean's skinny, sullen and struggling brother, who had followed Sean's path to the University of South Carolina but with less than stellar results. "They were close, though, and planned to work together to build their own business."

"I thought Daddy went to play football after college. Wasn't *that* his business?"

"That was the plan. Your dad was going to play pro ball as long as he could and pay off the mortgage while Jason managed the tourist cabin business without taking any money for it and worked for his family. Your dad planned to retire in Mt. Knott and they would then share the business." The covers made a soft rustling as Charity folded them back and tucked her feet up to sit cross-legged. "Only he got injured after only a few games and couldn't play anymore. And once Jason realized he'd have to fund the running of this place himself...well, I'm not exactly sure what happened between them, only that your dad never wanted to come back here after that."

Livie perched on the edge of the bed, hugging her pillow and chewing on her lower lip. She scrunched up her face in her classic "you're not off the hook yet, Mom, I'm still thinking about all this" expression.

Charity held her breath. She didn't want to go into all of Sean's issues with Olivia here and now. However, if the child asked a direct question, she would do her best to give a direct answer. "Does that answer your questions, Livie?"

The kid added rubbing her chin to underscore the extra-thinking going on inside her head.

"You know you can ask me anything, right?"

A nod. A distracted hum.

"You look like you're really puzzling something out." Charity swung her legs over the side of the bed and braced herself for anything. "So, ask."

Her only child lifted her somber, wise-beyond-her-years gaze to Charity, drew a deep breath and asked, "Can we eat breakfast out of the vending machines?"

Charity sat there stunned for a moment before she burst out laughing, reached out and drew her startled daughter into a hug. "Better than that, we can partake of an honest-to-goodness Carolina country cooking at a…" she tried to recall the exact words on the flyer from Mt. Knott's Chamber of Commerce she'd found on top of the TV last night "…quaint local eatery…home of pie so good you'll eat dessert first."

"Pie for breakfast!" Livie cheered and clapped. "C'mon, Mom, get dressed and be hasty about it, will ya?"

Chapter Six

"Hey, cool!" Livie made a beeline for the stools at the service counter at the charming little place called Josie's Home Cookin' Kitchen.

"Cool. The perfect word," Charity murmured. That's what she needed to stay and that's how she should look at this whole experience. With a sense of wonder, even excitement, sure. But also a bit of calm detachment.

"Can I get pancakes *and* eggs *and* bacon, Mom? Lots of bacon? Can we sit here? These things spin!" Livie hopped on a chrome stool with a red padded cushion and took it for a whirl, literally.

Ordinarily Charity would have quietly but firmly told her daughter to stop but with no one around, not even a waitstaff at the moment, she decided to let the kid *be* a kid, just for a minute. "One good thing about sleeping in slightly, looks like we missed any early morning rush."

"More bacon for us, then," Livie cheered.

"What's with the bacon? You usually eat cold cereal and leave some in the bowl." In fact, Charity couldn't recall a time since Sean had died that Livie showed this much interest in a meal.

"Maybe the fresh air and hard work that made you sleepy makes me hungry," Livie suggested. "This is a great place."

The child might have a point. One Charity didn't want to fully acknowledge. Great place or not, Mt. Knott was just a stopover on their way…

For the first time since this all began Charity couldn't finish that sentence. She had always used terms like *new life* or *next phase,* but now it dawned on her that those euphemisms didn't actually say anything about her plans. Where was she headed after Mt. Knott?

She thought of the old saying about needing to know what you were running to rather than just what you are running from. She didn't know whether to blame her newly rested mind or the unrest that this experience caused in her emotions, but Charity suddenly found herself having to push down the rising tide of questions in order to stay on course with her plans.

That made her feel anything but cool.

"I think it's best if we take a booth, sweetie." A booth was cool. Especially one tucked away in a cozy, dark spot where she could sit back and observe without being the object of observation.

She did a surreptitious scan. Elevated booths lined one sun-washed wall, practically spotlighting would-be customers.

Not cool.

A self-serve coffee station cut into the space otherwise occupied by free standing tables.

Hardly cozy.

The service counter and cash register took up the length of the back of the room. Behind them, swinging doors stood ajar, showing part of the bustling kitchen and letting the aroma of baking pies waft out to the customers.

She inhaled deeply then shook her head and kept searching for a place where she could settle for a short time.

Finally she looked to the left. The whole wall sported black chalkboard paint from ceiling to floor with children's drawings on it, a spot for the daily specials and a good quarter section set apart by a drawing in colored chalk of a flowering vine with the words *prayer requests* above a long list of just that.

"Prayer," she said softly. There was something so compelling about a whole town that openly promised to pray for one another that she found herself drawn in that direction. This was exactly where she wanted to settle—for a short time.

"I don't think my aching back can handle a stool at a counter, honey," she called over her shoulder even as her eyes stayed on the empty booth by the wall. "So come on over here and join me for breakfast."

"Sure thing, darlin', but let me finish up with this first," came the deep voice practically double-dipped in a Carolina honey barbecue sauce of an accent.

Charity jerked her head up and to the right to meet a pair of eyes belonging to someone she had only just met yet had known most of her life. "Jason!"

"Morning, Miz Charity. How's every little thing with you?" He grinned.

"I, uh…" She didn't even try to finish that sentence. Just gulped and held her hands out in an ambiguous gesture.

That was cool, she thought sarcastically.

"Okay, then. You go on and get settled and I'll join you for breakfast as soon as I get this done." He raised one of the chairs he had in his hands but did not pause as he strode to the center of the restaurant. He plunked the chairs down where several tables had been pushed together to form one long eating space.

"Breakfast? I didn't…" Another nondescript gesture to try to get her point across.

"You sure did." He moved to a stack of chairs on a cart he must have just brought into the room when she had her attention fixed elsewhere. He yanked two more off it and went to the table. "You said I should join you over there for breakfast."

"She meant me," Livie called out.

When Jason glanced her way, the girl waved with

all the subtlety of a long-lost castaway on a deserted island signaling a circling rescue plane.

"She didn't mention any names," Jason teased, then aimed his steady eyes toward Charity. "I think she planned on having breakfast with me."

"How could I have planned that? I didn't know you'd be here." *In person.* He had, in many ways, been with her all morning in her thoughts, in her deliberations and even in her dealings with her daughter.

Now, seeing him standing right in front of her made her freeze in her tracks. The morning sun shining through the big windows highlighted the combed-once, constantly rumpled quality of his hair. It glared off the freshly pressed white cotton of his dress shirt, accentuating the broadness of his shoulders. It even seemed to brighten everything around him as he went about the simplest tasks with good-natured ease.

He *so* belonged in this community. It was a part of him, he a part of it. Had she ever felt that profound a sense of belonging? Of course she had, with the family who had taken her in when her own world had fallen apart, the O'Clares.

Emptiness and longing for home swept over her, but quickly ebbed when she looked into Jason Burdett's eyes.

"I didn't plan on being here myself but there was he-man grunt work to be done." He spread his arms out to indicate the table where he had just deposited the chairs. "So I was summoned."

We need some serious muscle. Livie's words came back to Charity and she responded to him with those in mind. "Summoned? To do what, play pack mule?"

He smiled, bent and grabbed up two chairs with each hand this time and lifted them easily. "Just one of the many services I provide."

"I believe you," she said softly.

"You should. I feel compelled, as you seem to have only seen me in my pack mule capacity, to let you know that I am a vice president of a growing regional industry."

"I'm duly impressed." And she was. "They don't give those out to just anybody."

"Not unless you're born into the family who owns the business," he said, clearly trying to beat her to the punch line that he expected to hear.

"I'm sure you earned it," she said in all sincerity. "You're not just a hard worker. You're a quick thinker with an even temper and a kind heart. In my opinion, any business would be…"

He tensed, anticipating the word she would use.

"…absolutely foolish not to have you on board."

He thanked her overtly for not calling him lucky by tipping his head. Still, the intensity in his eyes really drove home how much he appreciated her not using the *L* word about him or his job. "All this mule work does leave a fellow hungry, though. So how about it?"

Maybe she *had* been too hasty. Jason Burdett was strong, kind and accommodating to everyone. Even to quaint local eateries. Obviously he had not singled her out for that brand of special treatment, nor did he just act at his family's beck and call. What could it hurt to have breakfast with him?

"I'll be sitting over there," she said, indicating the booth by the prayer list with a dip of her head.

"'Kay." He dipped his head, too, and in doing so created a sense of intimacy between them, of two people sharing a secret, seeing no one else in the whole room for that briefest moment when their gazes met.

He hoisted up the chairs and moved to the long table again.

Charity put her hand over her heart fluttering high in her chest and forced her eyes to fix on Livie to call her over to the booth.

"Well, hello." A pretty young woman, with her golden curls caught up in a topknot and bib apron barely concealing her unmistakable baby bump, spoke to Livie from the serving side of the counter. "You traveling through town on your own or are you meeting your husband here for coffee?"

"I'm not married." Livie giggled and swiveled back and forth on the stool, her tennis shoes bumping and thumping as she kicked her feet. "And I'm not allowed to ride my bike off my street without a grown-up so I can't travel by myself!"

"So just coffee then?" The woman kept up her somber-faced ruse by flipping over the coffee cup on the counter.

"No!" Livie's hand shot out as though she seriously thought the woman would grab a pot and start pouring. "I can't drink coffee!"

The woman put her fist on her hip. "Then are you sure you should be in here alone?"

"I'm not alone. I'm with…" She did an energetic half-spin in Charity's direction, her arm out and finger pointing.

Charity took a step toward her child. "She's—"

"She's with us, Josie," Jason called out as he tucked the last chair into place at the table. "Can you accommodate her there at the counter?"

"Absolutely." The woman Jason called Josie smiled at Livie then put on a stern face for him. "But don't think that bringing guests will get you out of this meeting. You already skipped once. Skip twice and people will start to nominate you for stuff."

"What? A meeting?" But the woman and Livie already had their heads together over a menu.

No wonder the place looked deserted. Charity whipped her head around to look at Jason. "I don't want to intrude. If you have business to attend to—"

"It doesn't matter." He went to the coffee station, held up a carafe to ask if she wanted a cup.

She nodded.

"Even if I ran that meeting myself, recognized only my own suggestions and gaveled every other human being in the room into silence, they'd still nominate me for stuff." He proceeded to pour them each one then held up the creamer and sugar, to which she nodded again. "They just feel better about it if they pretend I could have avoided it some way."

"Maybe Livie and I should go." She started to scoot back out of the booth. "The hotel has vending machines. They even sell Carolina Crumble Patties. That will fill us up. If it doesn't, we can grab a snack before we go out to the cabins today."

"You think you can tackle all the work that needs doing out at those cabins on Crumble Patties and snacks?" He added cream and sugar to one cup and left one black. He popped plastic lids on them then brought them to the table just as she reached the edge of the bench. He did not physically cut off her exit but held her in place with a look and a quiet, "Stay…please?"

"Stay," she echoed. Suddenly there was nothing she wanted more. That simple thought scared her to the center of her being. All these questions, all these doubts, all the issues she left behind and all the ones she'd brought with her tugged her in a thousand different directions. "I don't think I should."

"Okay, then let me come with." He leaned in to set the coffees down. "Where you headed?"

"I don't…know." Her answer applied to his request, his question, her own state of mind. "But, I, uh, you have this meeting and…" *I have these feelings.* She tore her gaze from him before she blurted out something like that. "Livie, sweetie, c'mon, they're having a meeting here. We need to move on."

"But I just ordered, Mom. Bacon! Two kinds!" She held two fingers up. "Regular and Canadian!"

"It's okay. You are both welcome to stay," Josie said as she turned back from having put in the child's breakfast order.

"I don't want to be any trouble," Charity said when what she probably really meant was that she didn't want to *have* any trouble. Her course was set. But she had let her guard down and was in jeopardy of losing her cool.

"Look, if it will make you feel better, you and I can do a Mt. Knott power breakfast."

She jerked her head up. "A what?"

"Grab a couple of slices of pie and head to the park, which isn't really so much a park as a park bench in front of the church down the way. But it's shaded and we can talk and they can have their meeting."

"But Livie…"

"Josie?" He approached the counter.

The woman did not even look up at him but deftly wrapped up two large wedges of apple pie and popped them into a crisp white bag, which she handed to him with a sweetly smirking grin.

"Thanks." He gave Livie and wink. "You okay staying here, kid?"

"Did you not hear me say I'm getting *two* kinds of bacon?" She held her hands out and gave her head a shake that made her long, dark hair shimmy. "What's there to not be okay about?"

Jason grinned then nodded to Josie. "Watch yourself. She may stage an overthrow at your meeting and be running everything by the time we get back."

"I guess I'm outvoted. Maybe we can make this a working breakfast and stop at the hardware store to pick up supplies?" That mere suggestion of establishing a plan eased the tightness in her chest. She gathered up the coffee cups and marched toward the door.

"Be good, Mom!" Livie called out.

Charity's cheeks flashed with heat. She caught a glimpse of her reflection in the glass front door. Her cheeks had definitely gone pink. Then she caught Jason standing direction behind her, studying that same reflection.

"I'll keep an eye on your mom, Liv," Jason promised.

"Oh, we know you will!" Josie called back.

The pink in her cheeks rose to enflame her whole face and turn it almost as red as her hair.

Jason pushed open the door.

Charity glanced back at her child, then at Josie, then at the prayer list. She did not look at Jason but felt his presence near her. Her gaze rested on the prayer list again.

"Enjoy yourself, sweetie," she called out as they moved onto the sidewalk. "It is, after all, only for a short while."

Chapter Seven

"This meeting, is it important?" Charity asked.

The door fell shut with a woosh that sent a puff of chilled air up Jason's back.

Or maybe that was just his response to the thought of trying to explain his family's expectations to one of the few people in the world who held him entirely apart from the Burdetts.

"It's just about Heritage Days and what humiliating thing they want me to do to help celebrate them." He held his arm out to get her moving. He didn't have much time to spend with her before she headed out to the cabins again, and didn't want to spend it standing in front of a place where his family planned to gather soon.

"What *are* Heritage Days?" She paused to hand him his coffee cup, then tear off the plastic tab on her own cup's lid so she could take a sip.

"Pretty much what it sounds like." He started them down the sidewalk, one eye out for the broken parts so he could steer her away from them. Without letting her know he was steering her away, of course. "It's a week set aside to commemorate the past."

"Commemorate the past?" She gave a derisive snort. "It figures I'd show up in a place doing something like that when all I want is to forget the past and move on!"

Move on he'd gotten from her, but wanting to forget the past? News to him. He peeled back the perforated plastic tab on his coffee lid. Steam, rich with the aroma of the last of the carafe's brew, rose up to engulf his nose.

He lifted his cup to his lips and shifted only his eyes to study Charity O'Clare's lovely face. Yesterday he'd made a point of memorizing those features. He had seen strength in the set of her chin. Courage and caring shone in those deep brown eyes. Her playful sense of humor never strayed far from the ready upward curve at the corner of her lips. Determination and drive, he'd found those in her every effort. And pain, he'd caught glimpses of that in her reactions, the way her gaze flickered away sometimes, unable to meet his.

All this he had committed to memory, but today he realized he had missed something. Fear.

Charity O'Clare was terrified. Of what, he might never know. He doubted she would ever volunteer the information. What could Jason do about that? Nothing except promise himself here and now that he would not add to anxiety.

All sorts of conversation starters went through his head. He finally went with, "So, watcha lookin' for in a—"

"I'm not. All right?" Her gaze flitted away from him again. "I came here to put my property on the market, not myself."

"Door lock?" He chose to politely ignore her outburst and finish his actual question.

"Door…lock?" she murmured, then let out a self-deprecating groan. "You want to hand me my piece of pie now?"

He raised the bag. "Hungry?"

"Not really, but at least if I have a mouthful of pie, it might keep me from saying something stupid for a few minutes."

He withdrew his offer of the pie in the to-go bag by lowering it and shaking his head. "You're doing okay."

"Am I?" Her whole posture picked up.

"Yeah." He did not start walking again but stood there on the sidewalk at the town's lone traffic light and studied her, his head cocked. "A little defensive, but then I, of all people, should understand that. Right?"

It was the perfect opportunity for her to bring up Sean and the past. To let them talk in earnest and maybe, just maybe resolve some of the old hurts. If only she would open up to him.

Trust me, he said with his posture, his eyes,

everything but his voice. *Let down your guard and let me help.*

"You call it defensive. I call it—" The cell phone in Charity's pocket cut her off. "Excuse me."

She reached for it, checked the small screen then clenched her jaw. She raised her eyes to the red light. The phone chimed out again.

"I have to take this." She shut her eyes and, before he could ask her if she needed some privacy, she answered, "Hello, Mother O'Clare."

Her knuckles went white where they curved to grip the small phone. Her voice tightened as the fear he had seen in her earlier crept over her features again.

But fear of what? Surely, not of her in-laws.

"No. I know I promised to call every day. I just got busy and… Yes, Livie is fine. I don't know why Davey isn't answering his phone."

"Bet you could hazard a guess why he's not," Jason muttered with a teasing grin, trying to lighten things up just a little.

"They want to help." She lifted her weary gaze to him, lowered the phone slightly and whispered, "They *always* want to help…with everything…all the time."

Which was why Charity fought so hard to do things her way, without interference from anyone…from *him*…he concluded.

"Yes, we're eating properly," she said, rejoining the fairly one-sided conversation already in progress.

"I know a vacation is no excuse for… Okay, okay, go get Pop O'Clare. I'll wait."

"Vacation?" he asked softly. "They don't know why you're in Mt. Knott, do they?"

"They don't know I *am* in Mt. Knott," she corrected, then turned her back on him just as she faced a barrage of new questions and suggestions from her father-in-law. "Yes, I have enough money. No, I won't."

The light changed. She charged across the street and down the sidewalk with the phone to one ear and her eyes on the ground.

"The church is that way." Jason pointed down the side street to his right.

"We're okay on our own." Charity kept going. "No! We do not need you and Mother O'Clare to join us for the weekend!"

"Or we could do it your way," he said quietly. He headed after her, but a quick glance to the side as he passed the new bait shop stopped him cold. "Hey, I think I know that walleye!"

"Shh." She pressed the phone to her shoulder and glared at him.

He put his hands on her shoulders and turned her slowly toward the window of the newly opened shop.

Her newly sunkissed face went totally pale. She raised the phone slowly to her ear. "I have to go, Pop. I'll call you tomorrow."

She ended the call and slid the phone back into her pocket. She took a step toward the window of the old gas station where local characters Jed and Warren had hung a Heritage Days Bass Lake Fishing Tournament Entry Forms Here sign between two mounted fish, one of them with a full set of dentures in its mouth. "That's the fish I tried to hit you with!"

"What's all this ruckus about?" Warren, dressed in blue-and-white striped overalls and a tan fishing cap squashed down over his wiry gray hair came trundling up to the front door and leaned out.

Jed crowded in behind him. "Did I just hear you say you hit Lucky Dawg with a fish, young lady?"

"Not just *any* fish. *That* fish!" She stabbed her finger at the one in the window.

Both men's heads turned to eyeball the plaques.

"That fish was at my cabin yesterday. It was stolen!" She looked at the two men. "You bought a stolen fish."

"I thought you said you threw it away," Warren said.

"Threw it *at me*," Jason corrected. "We left both of those on the front porch of the main cabin at Twin Cabins Lake."

"One of your workmen picked them up." Warren sounded pretty sure about that.

"Skinny kid? Dark hair?" Jed held his hand out to indicate someone just a little taller than Charity and about five inches shorter than Jason. "Told us you said we might be interested in buying these."

"He used my name?"

"Yep. 'Lucky Dawg says,' he says."

"I didn't have any workmen at the cabin," Charity

told the two men. "So whoever you got that from had to have been there on the porch when Jason suggested I sell the old trophies to you."

The little sneak couldn't have been more than a few feet away from Charity, from Liv. It made Jason's blood boil to think of it. However, he didn't want to scare Charity. He had to buy himself some time to think this through. "Not necessarily. Everyone in town knows me."

"And 'tween us, *we* know everybody in town." Jed slapped Warren across the upper arm. "Didn't know this fellow, though."

"He might be back." Warren scratched the back of his neck. "Said he knew where he could get some more like these."

Pale and wide-eyed, Charity turned her face to Jason. "He's going back to the cabins."

"Then so am I." Jason looked at the men first, then Charity.

"Oh, no, I can't ask you to do that. I'll call the sheriff and tend to this myself." Charity held her coffee cup so tightly the foam squeaked in her palms. "You have Heritage Days responsibilities, after all."

"Responsibilities?" Jed barked out a laugh. "Is that what you call letting your family dress you up in the duds of some phony ancestor and ride on the back of a flatbed and throw Crumble Patties?"

"I say one year throw them all for a loop and show up dressed like Gravy Joe." Warren laughed.

"I'd ask who Gravy Joe is, but that might imply I plan to stick around long enough to listen to your explanation." Charity looked from Jason to Jed and Warren. "Can I get a few supplies here?"

She wasn't thinking clearly. Jason wanted to step in and do her thinking for her. Yes, that's the very thing that had her running from the O'Clares, but this was different. This was him. Helping was what he did. "You'll still need to hit the hardware store, too."

"I know," she snapped. She rubbed her temple. "I also need to find a sitter for Livie and call the sheriff's department."

"I can arrange for one of my sisters-in-law to watch Livie."

"Josie," she said softly. "She's your sister-in-law, isn't she?"

"One of them."

"Yes. Okay. Do that, please." She said it as if she were the one who came up with the idea and had given the order.

If that's what it took to get her to accept his help, Jason had no issues with that. He'd been ordered about by bossier women with far less need of his services. "Consider it done. Anything else?"

Trust me. He did not say it. Instead, he gave her no other option. "This is my obligation, Charity. To make sure you stay safe. For Sean."

"Okay, but let's hurry. The little thief might already be out there robbing me blind."

Chapter Eight

Guard up. Face the direction you intend to go. Stay on course.

Charity had repeated those reminders over and over as she and Jason picked up the new lock and other supplies at the small, grit-covered hardware store in Mt. Knott. She nearly let them fall by the wayside when she watched Jason interact with his sister-in-law as they made arrangements for Livie. Then on the drive out to the lake and for the past half hour as they went about their work, she had found herself practically humming them under her breath. Especially as Jason tackled his chores around the old cabin with good humor and hard work.

It was the phone call that did it, she told herself. Rattled her right down to the core.

The O'Clares had that effect on her. They overwhelmed her with their good intentions and since

Sean's death, with their attention, which she sus-pected was their way of dealing with their grief. She wanted to be sensitive about that but feared that if she didn't find a way to break away from them she'd lose herself and never make her own way in the world.

Still, they were good people who only wanted the best for her and she loved them so much…

Guard up. Face the direction you intend to go.

She raised her head from the work that had con-sumed her for the past half hour here on the lakefront by the main cabin. Her gaze locked directly on Jason Burdett.

Stay on course.

She shook her hair back and stepped aside to show him her handiwork, holding a paintbrush out at arm's length to keep red paint from dripping on her shoes. "There."

"No trespassing?" Jason folded his arms and rubbed his knuckle over his chin. "You think a crummy sign is going to scare off someone seen stalking around here for weeks and has now stolen from you?"

"No, I think it will give me some legal ground to stand on in regards to, well, the ground I'm standing on." She sounded every bit as petulant and even more pouty than Livie had when they had told her she couldn't come out to the cabins today. She set the paintbrush down, whirled around and nabbed her sign up. "And my sign is not crummy."

Taking a few steps, she planted the yardstick in the

ground. It sank in less than an inch, then wobbled and leaned to one side.

"Here, let me—"

"I can do it," she snapped, snatching up a rock to pound the makeshift stake into the dark, damp dirt. Then, feeling guilty at her curtness, she added, "If you really want to make yourself useful, you can start painting more signs. I plan to stick them up everywhere."

He grumbled.

She pretended to ignore his grousing by thwacking the top of the yardstick with her sign attached to it. But as she raised the rock again, she did look under her arm to try to steal a peek at him.

The large man knelt on one knee over the board, his back to her. "You only have enough to make a few signs here, you know."

"Then I'll use whatever I can find to make more." She made a sweeping motion with her hand to include the lake and cabins and path and road. *Her* cabin, *her* lake, *her* path and road. For the first time today she felt truly in charge of the situation. "Thanks to your friends I have plenty of posts."

"If Jed and Warren had known how you planned to use those, I don't think they'd have given them to you." He dipped his brush into the thick red paint.

"Why not?" She slung the bright yellow and neon orange yardsticks over her shoulder and scanned the horizon for the best places to post more warnings. She was finally taking action.

"Because you're putting one of the best fishing spots on all of the Bass Lake area off-limits and right before the big tournament." The brush went slashing along in his hand. "Couple fellows just opened a bait shop and might take that a little personal."

"I don't even know those guys," she argued. "How could it possibly be personal?"

"Like it or not, this place is part of the fabric of our community." He looked at her over his shoulder. "Of our history."

Sean's and mine. Sean's and yours. Now, yours and mine.

That's not how he intended it, she could tell by the way he frowned after the words came spilling out. Still, that implication hung in the air between them.

Let it go, she wanted to say to him. *If you pretend that's not part of all of this, I won't challenge you.*

"You can't disregard that." He did not let it go. "You can't shut it out with a sign."

"That's just what I plan to do." Keep her guard up against the truth? A tall order but it could be done. "I plan to leave all of this behind me with a sign. One that reads Sold."

He dove back into this project. "Then what?"

She started to turn toward the lake, caught herself, then turned toward the road that led back to the highway and angled her chin up. "Then my life begins."

"So everything up to the point when you sell this property, that wasn't living?" he asked quietly, still writing on the board.

"My life." She put her hand over her heart, and kept her gaze focused on the road. "On my own."

"On your own?" He set the brush aside, took up the paint can and stood. He looked down at the sign, then at her, then in the direction she was facing. Finally, he moved into her line of vision and grinned slightly. "Don't tell me you're thinking of leaving Livie in Mt. Knott?"

"You know what I mean." She reached for the handle of the paint can and snatched it away from him. A few fat droplets of red went splashing around their feet but missed their shoes. "My life, Livie's life, without…you know."

He nodded and bent to retrieve the top of the paint can. "I just thought you usually say what you mean and you said…"

"Don't." She held her hand up. "You of all people should understand my feelings on this matter, as a man who just an hour ago invented an excuse to duck out on his own family."

"That's different. *My* family is going to do what they are going to do whether I am there or not. I don't really have much say or any sway over them. They call, I answer."

"I answered when the O'Clares called." Charity

could empathize but, looking at both of their situations, she had very little sympathy for the man.

"Your family, on the other hand, is close and caring and well-intentioned." He leaned over and pushed the lid down on the paint can dangling from her right hand. "They want what's best for you."

She wanted to tell him he was wrong, but she couldn't. "Yeah, they may be all those things but they are also insular, smothering, overbearing and think they know what's best for you, um, me."

"So we share a few of the same family issues." He held his hand out to take the can. "You just have a better thesaurus than I do."

"Poor baby. When you take the rest of those fish into the bait shop, which you should do as soon as the sheriff arrives, why don't you keep a few dollars and buy a…" She glanced down at the sign he had just painted. "Buy yourself a dictionary, Jason!"

"Did I misspell trespassing?"

She swooped down and grabbed up the sign, holding it high for him to see as she read aloud, "Violators will be *persecuted?*"

His grin grew broad. "You've heard the saying? Write what you know."

She tossed the sign on the grassy slope in front of the cabin. "What *I* know is that if you plan to sabotage my efforts then I don't need your so-called help."

"So-called?" He huffed out a sharp laugh but clearly wasn't really amused.

"Don't get all touchy about it. I know in this town you're the 'go-to guy.'" She crooked her fingers to frame the phrase in invisible quote marks. "Everyone relies on you."

"Relies?" Another scoffing laugh, this one softer as though genuinely enjoying the irony of her words. "You *do* have a better thesaurus than me. Or a very different dictionary. In all my reference material, you look up Lucky Dawg Burdett you won't see 'go-to guy.'" He, too, made the invisible quotes. "You'd find the 'get him to do it' guy. No one relies on me. If all else fails, they resort to me."

It was the weariness in his voice that got to her. His sincerity as he shared his disappointment at the way he felt people saw him. She sighed and reached out, giving him a pat on the arm as she said quietly, "That may be under Lucky Dawg but under Jason Burdett I suspect you'd find a man people count on."

"Yeah?" He tipped his head to one side, the light returning to his piercing gaze. "*People* count on me, but you can't?"

She could not look at him. So she turned her head and found herself looking at the door he had fixed, then at the canoe he had rowed, the sign materials he had toted out for her and finally the man himself. "I never said I can't count on you. If I made you think that then—"

The sounds of a car's tires crunching over the rock-strewn road leading to the cabin cut her off.

"There's someone from the sheriff's department now." She glanced at his sign then clutched the yard sticks in her hand more tightly. "You don't have to stick around any longer. You probably have a lot to do."

He planted his feet firmly next to the No Trespassing sign. "I'll stay."

She sighed and tossed the yardsticks onto the ground.

A young man in a tan shirt, dark brown pants and sporting a ball cap with a badge insignia on it strode up to them.

"Heard y'all had some suspicious activity going on 'round here?" He stuck out his hand immediately to Jason. "Deputy Kirk Gosling."

"We've had reports of someone lurking around her for a couple of weeks but didn't have any evidence that they'd done anything until today." Jason did not respond to the offered hand, just jerked his head toward Charity. "This is who you need to speak with. The owner of the property."

"Charity O'Clare." She thrust her hand out, eager to regain control of the situation. "Thank you for coming out."

"My pleasure. I love this old place." Deputy Gosling turned, hands on his hips, his stance wide, and faced the lake. Even with his eyes hidden behind mirrored lenses Charity could tell he was taking in the panoramic view. And that view was taking him back to another time.

So before he could launch into a sentimental ramble, waxing nostalgic about father-and-son fishing trips, moonlit canoe trips, shared insights by the campfire, and all those kinds of things that were the exact opposite of the kinds of memories she hoped this place would allow her to provide for her daughter, she held her hand up. "Make me an offer and all this can be yours."

He turned to her and cocked his head. "You're selling it?"

"No offers yet." She wanted to make that clear. A local lawman might know just the right people to send her way for a fast and uncomplicated sale. "But it can't come as much of a surprise, the place has sat empty for years now. Except for whoever has been poking around here and stole my…stuff."

"Over two years? Been that long? And now you've got suspicious activity *and* theft?" He nodded slowly as he turned his head to take in the whole scene—cabins, canoes, lake. "Well, there's your problem."

"Are you saying that I'll have a hard time selling a commercial property that seems to have lost its vitality?" She hadn't thought of that but it made sense.

"No, ma'am, I'm saying that as long as nobody's out here, it looks like fair game for everyone from vandals to homeless folks to thieves."

"Vandals and homeless and thieves?"

"Oh, my." Jason leaned in and murmured in perfectly timed counterpoint, à la *The Wizard of Oz,* to her concerns.

"Don't make fun." She had to fight not to smile at his gentle teasing.

"I'm not making fun." He straightened his back and wriggled his shoulders the way a man does when he's just finished with some manual labor or wanted to shake off an unseen burden. "I just think that as problems go, it's a pretty easy fix."

Gosling shrugged. "Just have someone stay out here."

"If it was just me…" Charity looked up at the main cabin. "But there's Livie to consider."

Jason ran his hand back through his shaggy blond hair and sighed. "I'll stay."

"I can't ask that of you." She couldn't *ask* it of him, but deep down what she wanted to say but couldn't bring herself to blurt out was "thank you." "I can't let you do it."

"You didn't ask. And it's not your place to let me do or not do anything." Jason smiled down at her. "I'm telling you I'll stay."

"But it's *my* property." If she let him do this, it would only muddy her emotional connection to him and this place. "I should be the one."

"So you both stay." Gosling readjusted his ball cap then hooked his thumbs in his belt loops. "Two cabins. Two people. Twice the pairs of eyes and ears. Besides, the more activity around the area the less likely someone will come sneaking around."

"The more work we can get done," Jason concluded.

"And the more viable it looks to someone wanting to buy the place," Charity had to admit.

"Sure a lot better than those crummy signs." The young man frowned in the direction of Charity's still-dripping No Trespassing warning.

She started to protest the term for a second time today when a swift breeze blew up from across the lake. The board swayed.

Crack.

The yardstick snapped in half.

"Crummy sign," she muttered.

Guard up. Face the direction you want to go. Stay on course. Make peace with the past. Move on.

Charity considered her ever-growing list of things she had to do before she got to do what she had planned to do. She couldn't really do any of those things until she sold this land. She couldn't sell this land until she got rid of the thief and got the cabins in shape.

She could not do any of that alone. She thought of the prayer list at Josie's. Nobody really ever did anything alone, did they? She shut her eyes. She said a quick prayer for strength.

Then she opened her eyes and looked directly at her very own—temporary—"go-to guy." "Okay, Jason, which cabin do you want, and how long can you stay?"

Chapter Nine

"Hey, Josie! What can you hook me up with in terms of eats? I need a couple days' worth of stuff that won't spoil in a cooler and doesn't need any fancy prep stuff. You know, like having to cook it."

"There's a new invention everyone's talking about." Josie's husband, Adam, the head honcho of the family business, turned slowly on the stool at the counter. "It's called a grocery store. You ever hear of it?"

"Heard of them but haven't seen one in about a few years." About the time the Crumble first started having its financial downturn and the whole town, including the cabins at Twin Cabins Lake, started feeling the pinch.

"Don't mind your big brother." Josie came out from the kitchen with a plate in each hand. She set one in front of Adam then whirled away to take the other one to a customer at a nearby table.

The aroma of pie and meatloaf and mashed potatoes threaded throughout the room. Jason's mouth watered. He ate at Josie's at least seven times a week. Sometimes, twice that. He glanced around him at the tables, the familiar faces, the prayer list on the wall.

As Josie hurried back to the kitchen, she called out cheerily, "I'll see what I can pull together."

"Thanks." Jason plunked down onto the stool next to Adam's and gave the shorter, dark-haired man a grunt.

Adam scoffed over his raised coffee cup.

For the brothers this was practically a whole week's worth of interaction.

"Yep. Don't mind your older brother, but you might want to have a word with your boss." Adam lowered his coffee cup and gazed into it.

Jason thought about making a smart remark about Adam admiring his own reflection but thought better of it. "My boss knows where to find me if he needs me."

"Not in your office," Adam muttered. "Maybe your boss wonders why you don't see fit to at least pretend to owe him an explanation for all the work you missed this week. Maybe clear it with him about any other time off you plan to take."

Jason reached out and flipped over a coffee cup then slid it in front of him. He didn't really want caffeine this late in the day but he felt compelled to do *something* as he said in a low, malcontent tone, "We both know nobody needs me at the Crumble."

"Busy time." Adam said it clearly as a contradiction.

"Are you kidding me?" Jason rolled his eyes.

"Heritage Days," Adam mumbled just before he finally put his cup to his lips.

"Ah, I get it." Jason pushed the empty coffee cup in front of him away and gave a soft but acerbic laugh. "With me otherwise occupied, Josie and Dora are roping you and Burke into the plumb jobs you normally pawn off on me."

"Hey, as Vice President of Special Projects, you—"

"Yeah. I know." He held his hand up. "I get paid a whole lot of money to pretty much do what nobody else wants or has time to do. Lucky me."

"No such things as luck." Adam set the cup down hard then turned to his brother, his eyes narrowed. "There's work. There's results. There's choices. There's consequences."

Jason took that in, then leaned against the counter with both forearms, his hands folded together. "If we weren't brothers and I didn't actually own as big a stake in the Crumble as you do, I might take that as a warning about the status of my job security."

"Told you I wasn't talking to you as your brother now." Adam looked straight ahead.

Jason followed his line of vision and caught a glimpse of Josie hustling happily around the kitchen.

"Work. Results. Choices. Consequences," Jason

murmured mostly to himself. Nobody needed him at work. The only results his job netted? A paycheck for him, one that he didn't really need. And an easy out for his family.

He'd made that choice years ago. Regret and a lack of purpose in his life, his consequences.

"What about…" Jason looked from the kitchen to the prayer board "…other things?"

"What other things?" Adam practically snarled at his younger brother.

Jason tipped his head in Josie's direction. "What about love? What about faith? What about hope and second chances?"

Adam took only a moment to consider, not even looking at his wife or raising his head to take in their surroundings. "There are elements of work and choice in those things, too."

He had intended to ask his brother if he believed in those less tangible ideals. But as Jason considered a moment, he supposed he'd gotten his answer. Or all the answer he required.

He stood, his mind made up, and stretched out his hand to Adam.

"Here you go, Jason." Josie breezed back into the dining area just then, holding a large brown paper bag with handles on it, with fresh veggies sticking out of the top and emitting from its depths the delicious sweet and tangy smell of hot fruit pie. "This should hold you over a while—some assembly required.

Oh, and if you plan on staying at the cabins, you really should take along—"

"Worms! A whole tub of big, fat, squirmy worms!" Livie burst through the door of Josie's holding a whole plastic container up and out.

"You know, it's easier to get a meal for a big-mouthed bass in this town than to get enough non-snack-food type groceries to feed a family in this town." Charity breezed in after them.

Adam swiveled ever-so-slightly on the stool to glance behind him and muttered for Jason's ears only, "Well, well, here comes a couple of those 'other things' you mentioned earlier, eh, little brother?"

"You don't actually feed fish worms, you know, not like tossing bread crumbs out to birds or peanuts to squirrels," Josie informed Livie as she pushed the bag of supplies across the counter toward Jason.

"Oh, I know." Livie spoke with the air of authority worthy of a professional outdoorsman. "We didn't get these to feed the fish. We got 'em to *catch* the fish."

Charity looked up at Jason a bit apologetically. "She got it in her head that she's going after Ol' Turkey and *you* are going to help her."

Charity fought accepting his help at every turn but he had to give her credit. She did not impose her own issues and fears on her bright-eyed child. On Sean's child.

Jason grinned at the kid. "Looks like I have my work cut out for me, then."

"Looks like you have your *choices* laid out for you." Adam put his hand on Jason's shoulder, a reminder of both of their roles in the family and at the Crumble.

"That's where you're wrong, big brother." Jason gave Josie a smile, then slid Adam's hand away. "I'm putting my stock in those *other things*."

"Which means?" Adam scooted forward on the stool as though about to stand up and bump chests with his taller and more athletic younger brother.

"Which means that I've made my choice." This time Jason put his hand on the other man's broad shoulder and smiled. "You can't tell me what to do anymore, Adam. I quit."

Chapter Ten

"Just like that?" Charity ran after the man who had just tossed his career aside like a used paper napkin, then strolled casually out the door carrying a delicious-smelling paper bag.

He stepped onto the sidewalk and paused.

She and Livie made it outside. The door fell shut.

Without a word he started walking, head held high, toward her SUV. "Do you mind taking these out? I need to swing by my house and pick up a change of clothes and a toothbrush."

Charity rushed after him. "Jason! What are you thinking?"

"That I like to change my underwear every day and avoid tooth decay?"

Livie giggled at his response and hurried to keep pace with his long-legged stride.

Charity did not find anything about all this funny.

She also didn't see any point in hurrying away from the scene of the...whatever that was...when she knew the instant he came to his senses he'd have to march right back to his brother and set things right.

"Stop right there." She held her ground on a bit of sidewalk just out of view of the windows of Josie's Home Cookin' Kitchen. "And talk to me. Why did you do that? Why did you up and just like that..." she snapped her fingers "...quit your job?"

He kept walking away. "Some people act and *then* think. Others think for years before they act. In the end, to the casual bystander, they both look like a choice made..."

He reached her SUV, turned and met her gaze then snapped his fingers, too. "Just like that."

She couldn't make herself take another step. She'd walked in during the brothers' conversation but she did not have to have heard every word to know that Jason had acted, or *re*acted, hastily. He'd missed work for two days and skipped an important family meeting and who knew what else because of her.

Didn't he understand? She did not want to be the reason behind his failure, as she had been with Sean. "But what are you going to do?"

"Go out to your cabins and help you." He set the bag on the hood of her SUV and held is hand out. "If you'll hand me the keys now, I'll get this stuff loaded and we can roll."

"C'mon, Mom." Livie held her bait tub. "I can't hold this forever."

"Yeah, Charity. C'mon, you don't really want to stand out here on the sidewalks of Mt. Knott and risk opening this can of worms, do you?"

"It's a plastic tub," Livie corrected.

"Your mom knows what I mean." He shifted his eyes to catch her gaze.

Charity tensed, suddenly aware of how public even a small town could seem. A town so close they prayed for each other probably wouldn't have any problem stopping everything to enjoy the spectacle of Lucky Dawg Burdett and the owner of Twin Cabins Lake shouting their personal business out in the open for all to hear.

Charity yanked her keys out of her purse and hustled to join them. She pressed the remote lock to allow Livie to get inside, then motioned for Jason to meet her at the back window.

"Help me? You want to help me?" When he reached her, she pressed another button and the rear window hatch unlatched with a pop. "Don't you mean help yourself?"

He scowled as he reached for the handle and lifted it to put the bag inside. "Help myself to what? I totally get that you are not interested in me, if that's what you mean."

"It's not and…" She had never said she wasn't interested in him, but that she wasn't interested in anything that took away from her ultimate goal. It was not a distinction she cared to argue right now, though. "And anyone can see you want to hightail it out to my cabins to get out of the line of fire."

"Hightail it?" He set the bag in the back then shut the hatch with a solid *wham* before turning to her, his amusement shining in his eyes. "What am I, part of a gang of desperados?"

"Oh, that's right, you're *not* part of a gang of desperados." She was pushing him but better to push and get him to undo what he had just done than to live with more questions and guilt. "You're a member of a wolf pack of brothers. Maybe I should have said you want to run off with your tail between your legs."

Too far? She had overstepped her bounds. She had known about this man for a good portion of her life, but to him she was a mere stranger. A stranger who had played some part in the way his one-time best friend's life had gone awry.

He plastered his palm against the glass. He lowered his head.

She bit her bottom lip to keep from blurting something else out and making things worse.

"With my tail between my legs?"

She knew how much he hated that whole dog/dawg reference and yet she had deliberately used it as a means to try to prod him to his senses. She wouldn't blame him if she sent her off to deal with the mess about the cabins on her own. In fact, she fully anticipated just that.

"Charity. Charity. Charity."

She took in a breath, quick and sharp.

His grin broke slowly but once it started it spread until his whole face lit up. He shook his head and sputtered out a soft chuckle before meeting her gaze again and murmuring, "You are so cute."

That hit her harder than the impact of anything she had prepared herself to hear ever could. She stole a peek at Livie on her knees in the front seat with her hands on the headrest openly staring at them, then moved in close as though the child might overhear when she asked, "What?"

He put his hand on her back and guided her toward the street. "I know what you're doing."

She wriggled away from his touch and planted her feet firm before throwing her head back to look up at him. "I am trying to keep you from making an impulsive mistake that will cost you your career."

"I don't have a career, Charity, I have a job." His laughing eyes grew somber. "No, not even that, I have a title. That should come as no surprise to you."

"Everything that's happened the past few minutes has surprised me," she confessed.

A hint of humor returned to his expression. "Including me calling you out on how cute you are?"

"*Especially* that."

"Aw, c'mon, think about it." He took her by the

shoulders to better drive his point home. "You don't really care if I resign my title as Vice President of Special Projects for the Carolina Crumble Pattie Snack Cake International Incorporated, do you?"

"Well, I…"

He lowered his face so that their foreheads almost touched, creating a private space for only the two of them. He spoke slowly, deliberately and honestly. "What really has your engine revving is the idea that I might have just caused a rift with my family."

No, her real fear was that *she* had caused a rift in his family. She just couldn't live with that. "They depend on you."

"They lean on me. It's not the same."

"Tell that to someone who doesn't have anyone to lean on," she whispered, taking her eyes off him to look out at the empty sun-dappled street.

"I am." He crooked his finger under her chin and physically drew her attention right back to him. "Leaning on someone isn't such a bad thing but it does imply that one day the leaner is going to have to stand on his or her or their own."

"Why do I think that lesson had nothing to do with you and the Burdett wolf pack and their wives?"

He smiled and straightened up, looked both ways, then gave her a nudge toward the door on the driver's side of the SUV. "In the end, Charity O'Clare, it turns out you aren't as big on breaking family ties as you want people—including yourself—to believe. You might want to think a while on that."

Charity did *not* want to think on that.

She did not want to think on it as she swept the cabin.

She did not want to think about it as she pulled down the dusty tattered drapes.

She did not want to think about it as she inflated the air mattresses she had brought for herself and the smaller single-size pink one—which was, in truth, a swimming pool float raft—for Livie.

She was still *not* thinking of it in a way that kept it popping up to the forefront of her thoughts every few minutes, as she cleared the kitchen table for dinner and suddenly realized she only had junk food to feed her child.

And that's how she came to finally think about the thing she had tried all day not to think about.

The O'Clares were probably sitting down to a wonderful meal about now. On days like this when Charity had come dragging home from whatever job she could find, she loved knowing that she and Livie would be well-fed.

Even when Sean was alive, especially toward the end when he had become so erratic and unhappy, they'd had to count on his parents for basic needs. The O'Clares had never turned them away.

She had thought that was part of the problem. If only they had said no to Sean. If only they had made him take responsibility for his life and the care of his family. But then, couldn't they say the same of her?

Without the money or time to go to college she had always just taken whatever work she could and had never stayed long at any one place to earn a promotion or seniority. That was because at least once a year Sean announced that he had a brilliant scheme and needed her to follow him at a moment's notice. But they never went anywhere. The schemes *or* the pair of them.

She looked down at the bare table, then at the sack of makeshift nourishment she'd collected from the motel vending machine and at the convenience store on the highway.

Was her trying to flee the O'Clares' influence that much different than Sean trying to outrun his own feelings of failure and inadequacy? She sank down into the chair. He stomach clenched. Her heart ached.

She had depended on the O'Clares all her life. Not simply leaned on them as she had told herself so often. *Depended upon them.*

They had never let her down. Regardless of how they might have done things differently with Sean, they had always been there for her. And for Livie.

And how was she planning to repay them?

"Mom, I take it back." Livie burst through the door. Her feet thundered over the old floorboards. The pink pool floatie squished by one corner in her small fist scuffed and bounced along behind her.

Above the sound of the door swinging to smack Jason in the shin, she shouted, "That motel is not the best place to stay ever. *This* is!"

"Oof!" Jason caught the door in one hand.

"When Jason gets the fire going—"

"*If* Jason gets the fire going," he corrected.

"*When*," Livie insisted, "he says we can roast weenies. That okay, Mom? Mom? Are you okay?"

Charity smiled even though she hardly felt like smiling. "I was just thinking about what we'd be having for dinner back home tonight."

"Maybe mush potpie," Livie suggested.

"What? What's that you said?" Jason put his hand to his ear.

"It's their version of shepherd's pie made with—"

He held his hand up to cut her off. "I meant what's that you called the place? Back *home?*"

She had. Meant it, too. "The O'Clares' will always be home to me, no matter where Livie and I land."

He nodded and came into the cabin, stepping over Livie, who had thrown the pool floatie down in the middle of the floor and done a belly flop onto it.

"Now, tell me about this, uh, mush potpie?"

"Kathleen O'Clare makes it with leftovers and Irish potatoes," Charity explained, grateful he hadn't so much as mouthed the words *I told you so* at her revelation.

"They specifically have to be *Irish* potatoes?" he asked.

Charity laughed, her mood lifted again. "In the O'Clare household *all* potatoes are Irish."

"They came to America because of the potato phantom," Livie offered.

"Famine." Charity corrected, scrunching up her nose at Livie.

Livie scrunched up not only her nose but also her whole upper body, and she put her fist over her mouth to hide a grin over the secret shared joke.

"They being the ancestral O'Clares, not Livie's Grandie and Grandpop," Charity said. Hey, she held Jason responsible for this wave of nostalgia about these people, he might as well learn a little about them in the bargain.

"*And* the Donnellys *and* the Finnegans," Livie quickly added.

He grabbed a chair, turned it around and sat in it backward as he asked, "The Who-ellys and the Who-egans?"

Livie smiled in delight as Jason's question.

"The Donnellys and the Finnegans," Charity said, a little humbled at the man's openness to their lesson in family history. "My mother-in-law was a Donnelly, and my maiden name was Finnegan."

"Charity Finnegan O'Clare," he said softly.

She'd heard it spoken so many times, but from his lips, it sounded like music.

"Can't get much more Irish than that, huh?"

She blushed. She just knew she blushed.

"My daddy used to say that they got chased to America by the potato phantom," Livie chimed in. The air mattress squeaked as she rolled onto her back. She stared at the ceiling as she said, "And he told me that if I ever forgot my Irish roots, the phantom would come for me, too."

"Your daddy was just being funny," Charity assured her child. Only suddenly, she didn't find the idea funny at all.

What is it that you called the place? Home?

You aren't as big on breaking ties as you want people—including yourself—to believe.

Some people act, then think. Some people think for years, then act.

Charity didn't know which she was. She didn't know where she had come from. She had even begun to question *who* she was.

"So, since we don't have mush potpie and the only thing Irish around here seems to be roots—" Jason winked at Livie then slapped his leg and stood "—who wants a hot dog?"

Finally! A question she could answer. Charity thrust her hand up. "I do!"

Jason's mouth crooked up on one side. "Okay, then, looks like I better get to work."

"Thanks," she called out as she watched him head for the door.

Thanks for making me think. Thanks for teaching me a thing or two and for not being too pig-

headed to learn something now and then. Thanks for being here.

"I just hope you know we can't pay you your usual salary," she joked instead of saying any of the things that passed through her mind as he glanced back at her.

He laughed and went outside, with Livie on his heels.

Charity sighed.

She'd only been on her own a few days and already her guard was down. She was emotionally and mentally twisted every which way. For now the only way for her to stay on course was for her to stay here and allow Jason to help her.

She was a mess.

In that moment sitting alone in this cabin that had played such a pivotal role in her late husband's life, Charity could no longer hide from her deepest fear. She was every bit as much to blame for Sean's downfall as his parents. And for all her brave talk about allowing Livie to seek her dreams, Charity had no idea how to do that for herself.

Chapter Eleven

"I have no job."

Jason struck a match.

"I left my job—correction, *jobs*—I'd had for a decade in a very unprofessional and decidedly unfamily friendly way."

He tossed the match onto the pile of twigs Livie had gathered to use as kindling to build a fire to cook their evening meal and waited. Nothing happened.

Livic lurched forward to prod the stack of sticks but Charity pulled her back, saying nothing.

Jason gave her an appreciative grin.

She gave him a steely-eyed look that he supposed meant she expected him to handle this the way she would—without accepting help. But when he met her gaze, the last thing on his mind was independence and self-sufficiency.

He dragged the head of another splintery wooden

match along the surface of the box. The smell of sulfur stung his nostrils. The fire warmed his fingertips. He dropped it into the pile at the center of the stone-lined circle set aside for campfires in front of the cabin. A flicker of flame.

He watched for it to grow as he said quietly, "I have an Irish cottage–style house nestled among the homes at the Burdett compound that I hardly ever really lived in, and now will be avoiding until at least after Heritage Days."

A crackle. A curl of white smoke rose from the sticks and wood. Then nothing.

"I guess it's official." He held his hands out and laughed. "I'm an unemployed homeless black sheep with no prospects."

He drew the clean spring air deep into his lungs and held it as he took in his surroundings. "And I don't think I've ever felt more relaxed and content."

"What about hungry?" Liv asked. "Have you ever felt more hungry? Because I don't think I have!"

"If you don't think you can get the fire going…" Charity stepped around her daughter with her hand outstretched toward the box of matches in his hand.

He waited until her fingers practically brushed the cardboard edges before flipping the box up in the air.

Her hand followed, reaching upward.

He nabbed her wrist, caught the falling box in his

other hand and used the momentum of her forward lunge to draw her close enough to him to whisper, "I never said I couldn't get a fire going, Charity."

Her cheeks went flame red. Her lips parted in an almost inaudible, "Oh."

"I have the skills." Still holding her wrist, he lowered her arm then smacked the box of matches into her palm. "I just need your permission."

"Oh…okay." Her wide eyes stayed trained on his face.

"Great." He let go of her, took a couple of steps and grabbed the No Trespassing signs she had painted.

Crack.

He broke them over his knee and tossed them into the circle.

Charity opened her mouth, supposedly to protest, but he swept the matches from her hand, knelt by the fresh kindling he'd just created and lit it.

The flame started low but spread rapidly and soon they had a roaring fire.

Both Charity and Livie praised him inordinately for that, which tickled him almost as much as it humbled him.

"I didn't do anything special," he told them.

Ever, he wanted to add.

They dined on a meal of hot dogs and roasted ears of corn courtesy of Josie and chips and soda from Charity's stash of junk food. Liv had wished for marshmallows and Jason made a note to make sure they had some tomorrow. She'd also wanted to stay up late and hear ghost stories, an idea her mother vetoed immediately, citing the fact that they had all had a long day and needed rest. Of course, Jason understood that the lurker turned thief they had come to protect the place against already had Charity's nerves on edge enough without some far-fetched tale of long-gone prom queens returning for a last dance or escaped killers on the loose.

So Livie settled for a few tall tales about Ol' Turkey that Jason had heard from Warren and Jed. When the flames subsided, Charity sent the child up to the cabin to get ready for bed, leaving the two of them alone by the glowing hot embers.

He did not dare let himself carry that thought any further. Both as a man of faith and as Charity's friend he had to keep his mind focused and his intentions honorable.

"Did I say I was content before?" He looked at her again. He had a full belly and, having spent the day and evening with Charity and Liv, a full heart as well. That should have been more than enough for him. "What I should have said was that I don't think I've ever been happier than I have been these past few homeless, jobless, nearly fireless few hours."

"I'm glad you waited until after Livie's bedtime to make that announcement." Charity shook her head. The radiance of the dying firelight glinted off her red hair and bathed her sweet face in shades of gold and smoky-blue shadows. "I'm going to have a difficult enough time setting a good example for her given my own unemployed, homeless, uncertain prospect status myself without you going and making it look so inviting."

"Inviting." He echoed her words and agreed with them, on his own terms. He scooted over a few inches toward where she sat on the cool grass. "You know what looks inviting to me?"

She put up her hand but did not shy away as he had expected her to. "Jason, we can't."

"We can," he said softly, moving closer still.

Her raised hand faltered. "We shouldn't."

At last they sat side by side, almost touching. "Why not?"

"Beeecau-zzzz..." She stretched the word out in an obvious ploy to buy herself time to think of a reason. She wanted to kiss him, too. She couldn't hide it, not that she was trying very hard to conceal it.

The guilelessness of her response drove all reason from his thoughts. Jason reached out and put his hand behind her neck, her thick, shining curls cascading over his fingers and knuckles. "Because?"

He gave her one last chance to protest.

She opened her mouth and inhaled.

He held his breath.

Da-dee-dee-dee. Da-dum-dee-dee. Dee-da-dee-dee-dum-dee-dee-dee.

The irritatingly recognizable opening notes of their newly revived Carolina Crumble Pattie jingle rang out from Jason's cell phone.

Charity jumped away from him and, as the silly tune went off again, started to laugh. "That's your ring-tone?"

The fire had died down so much by then that he could hardly make out her expression as he said, "My sister-in-law Dora came up with it as a gimmick and set our phones to do that when we get a call from a family member."

"Then maybe you should answer it." She drew her knees up to her chest and looped her arms over them.

Jason didn't have to be an expert in body language to know she had retreated from him.

Da-dee-dee-dee.

He freed the cell phone from the clip on his belt. As it chirped merrily through another chorus of what he had come to think of as his personal call to duty, he stared at the object. "You know, in movies, guys like me usually end up proving how much they've changed by throwing these in the lake."

"Don't you dare!" Charity lunged for it as though he had just threatened to toss a puppy or some actual live and cuddly creature into the depths. "With me and Livie here and you across the way tonight cell phones will be our primary means of communication."

Jason smiled and held the phone out of her reach, which made her lunge again, bringing her practically tumbling into his lap. "You're just giving me more incentive to toss this thing—so we'd have a reason to find a better means of communication."

The phone went silent.

"Like what?" She put her hands on his chest…and pushed herself upright and away from him. "Shouting across the river? Using some form of message with flashlights to signal we should each start paddling from one side and meeting in the mid—"

"Excellent idea," he said just seconds before he kissed her. Not a long, lingering kiss. That would have had her not just retreating but probably withdrawing all together. But his lips did brush hers lightly.

She relaxed in his arms, her fingers curling into the fabric of his cotton shirt.

He pulled away.

"Jason, we really can't…"

"We can." He ran his thumb over the fullness of her lower lip. "But we won't. I have too much respect for you, Charity, to try to convince you that you and I can have a future together. Not with me staying here and you trying to get away from here."

"I was thinking less about whether we had a future together and more about—"

"The past?"

She shook her head. "More about the way I think I have to behave, as Liv's mom and as a Christian."

"I see." He nodded and positioned his foot so that he could push himself up off the ground.

She grabbed the front of his shirt to keep him in his place. "That doesn't mean we can't sit here and talk. It's been a long time since I've just sat in the dark and talked to anyone that I wasn't trying to rescue or that wasn't trying to rescue me."

Jason settled himself back down next to her and laced his arm around her shoulders. "Talk all you want, then."

The lake lapped at the shore.

Now and then an ember popped.

The pines rustled.

Neither of them said a word.

Da-dee-dee-dee. The Carolina Crumble Pattie jingle started chiming again.

"Will they keep calling until you answer?" Charity sat up but kept her hand on his chest.

"No." Jason reluctantly took his arm from around her. "They'll keep calling until they get worked up enough to come out here to talk to me in person."

"Oh, great, just what we need." She threw her hands up, a gesture he felt as a rush of air and a blur of movement more than saw in the ever-dimming light. "An unsettling presence, a potato phantom *and* a wolf pack."

"With that much traffic, you'd think this place would be a financial gold mine."

Da-dee-dee-dee.

"Or at least draw an investigation by Scooby and the gang," she muttered.

Jason chuckled and flipped open his phone as it rang a third time. "R-hello."

Charity giggled softly.

His brother "Top Dawg" Burke, on the other hand, did not seem equally amused.

"Can't leave the girls hanging on this parade deal," came the gist of all Burke's barking.

Not, why did you quit your job? Are you okay? Not even an appeal to try to talk things through.

No, foremost on his big brother's mind was keeping his wife happy without having to get his own hands dirty.

Jason laughed. That was the real issue here. Burke was looking at having to take on the role of costumed float rider in the Heritage Days parade and he didn't like it. Not one bit. "Hey, you're a big dog. Straining against that leash a little?"

Burke blustered a nonreply to that.

"Stand up for yourself, man. Make it clear what you will and won't do." He looked at Charity, gave her a wink then concluded his encouragement for his brother to refuse to do his wife's bidding by adding, "Oh, and you might want to invest in one of those battery-operated pocket fans. Those venerable Southern ancestor costumes are hot!"

He had hardly hung up from Burke when Adam called, and then his younger brother, Cody.

He essentially told each of his brothers the same thing. Only each time he suggested a different costume and assured them it was the pick of the crop, the most comfortable, the least embarrassing, the best-looking.

"But don't tell the others you might wear the costume. Why give them time to give you grief over it?" Jason hung up on the last call and laughed.

"Why'd you do that?"

"Well, we don't want them fighting over who's the prettiest."

Charity leaned back, her arms straight and crossed her legs at the ankles. "You're really enjoying this, aren't you?"

"Actually, what I was *really* enjoying, before that onslaught of brotherly love and concern..." He put two fingers under her chin to turn her face toward his and her eyes on him alone.

"Did you see that?" She tore away from his touch and craned her neck to search the other side of the lake. "There!" She swung her arm out and pointed. "A light."

Jason jumped to his feet and searched the horizon from the walking path to the cabin across the way. "I don't see a thing."

"I did." She, too, scrambled to her feet. "I saw a light around the Camp Store Cabin."

"Probably a reflection from the fire." He put his hand on her upper arm to reassure her.

They both glanced down at the pile of ashes with only a few red and orange sparks left in it. His stomach clenched.

"We worked at both cabins all day." He spoke slowly and with calm detachment, even as his mind raced to make every connection possible to try to resolve this issue to his satisfaction. "No one could have gotten over there today without one of us seeing something."

"But I *did* see something." Her voice quivered. "Just now. A light."

He looked in the direction of the old abandoned cabin where he had intended to spend the night tonight. "It's not there now."

"I know." She stepped toward the shoreline. "It moved."

"Then maybe a set of headlights from a car?" He jerked his head toward the road that led to the highway and into Mt. Knott and beyond.

"I...I guess." She took a step toward him, then glanced back over her shoulder at the lake and the other cabin. "Probably."

"If it will make you feel better, when I go over to sleep tonight, I'll have a really good look around for anything suspicious." He tried to sound totally unconcerned by it all, but even the idea of someone out here with the girls on one side of the lake and him on the other had him on edge. He could handle this, of course. He would prove himself to her, but he would do it as someone who would not run rough-shod over her feelings and need for independence. "I probably ought to make sure that the last of this fire is out then head that way now anyway."

He turned to get the shovel so he could throw some dirt on the fire before he doused it outright.

Charity did not take her eyes from the other side of the lake. "I think we should call the sheriff."

He tried not to let her readiness to call out some-one else prey on his pride.

"Look, don't get all worked up. I'm here." He kept working. "We don't need to call the sheriff for something as insignificant as you thinking you saw a flicker of light."

"Oh, you're right. It would be ridiculous to call for a *flicker*." She turned and came around the edge of the fire circle where he stood, grabbed his arm and turned him around. "But that is no flicker!"

He'd totally not counted on her being right. His stomach knotted and he pushed her to get behind him. "Go to the cabin, stay low and quiet. When you get inside, call the sheriff. I'll stay here and keep on tending the fire to make it look as though we're going about our business here, totally unaware."

"Okay. Be safe," she whispered as she crept away.

Jason could only stand there pretending to carry on even as he went over and over in his mind what his attraction to Charity and his concentration on his own issues might have made him miss.

Too much, he decided. He sifted dirt around and kept his gaze fixed on the steady light burning in what looked like the large main room of the Camp Store Cabin. He had allowed his own feelings to rule over his commitment to help. He had acted like the Lucky Dawg that people suspected him of actually being—a guy who expected everything to turn out his way, that nothing bad would ever happen. He'd been the guy he had most feared he would become and now Charity and Liv might be in serious danger because of it.

Chapter Twelve

"Are you sure the light came from *inside* the cabin?" Deputy Gosling strode up to the main cabin, where Charity waited with Jason on the steps.

The light had come and gone a few times in the twenty minutes it took Gosling to get to them. By the time he had agreed to go around and look over the other cabin for himself, it had disappeared. Now, Gosling expounded on his theories of what caused the phenomenon people called a "ghost light" around here. Ball lightning, lightning bugs, faulty wiring in the old building, reflections off the lake, that kind of thing.

Charity stood there trying to not to lose her cool as she listened to the man question the very existence of the light at all. She thought back over these past few minutes, wondering if the man had ever really believed them. If he hadn't, did that mean she was on her own out here as far as the sheriff's department was concerned?

On her own. Charity gritted her teeth and tried not to let that rattle her too much. This was what she had wanted. What she had *said* she wanted. Now that conviction was being put to the test and Charity would rise to it.

She glanced Jason's way. Of course, it was easy for her to think that with Jason at her side. He hadn't wanted to leave her and Liv, even when Gosling asked if he wanted to ride along as he took the rugged walking path that Livie had walked along and where Charity had gotten her SUV stuck.

"You can go with him, you know," she had told him when she had come outside after checking on Livie.

"Can't." Jason had crammed his hands in his pockets and feigned a shudder. "Too scared."

"Yeah, right." She'd leaned against the column supporting the porch's roof, and had kept her eyes on the progress of Deputy Gosling's car moving slowly around the lake. "I think you just wanted to stay behind to see if you could steal some more kisses."

"Kisses? One kiss. But if you're offering more…" He'd taken a step toward her.

She'd held her hand up to bring him to a stop.

"Probably shouldn't have let our guard down anyway," she'd said, as much or more for herself than him. "We came out here to watch over the place."

Charity had wound her arms around herself. It

had grown cool after the fire had faded. The memory of that kiss and her responsibility to keep focused for Livie's sake had banked her inner fires as well. Guard up. Remain vigilant.

That's what she should have been doing, not—

"Pounding on the door, looking in the windows." Deputy Gosling's sharp tone brought her back from her momentary replay of the past twenty minutes. "Door was locked but I didn't see anything."

"You locked the door?" She looked at Jason.

"Told you I was scared," he quipped.

"Smart move. You've had reports of a possible vandal around. You have to take precautions. Exactly the kind of thing you'd think of, Lucky Dawg." Gosling gave Jason a walloping slap on the back.

"I was going to lock my door tonight," she murmured.

"Smart move on your part, too, ma'am." He tipped his head toward Charity as he headed for his car to leave.

She lifted her shoulders with pride.

"Having Lucky Dawg out here to watch over you," the deputy went on as he opened the door and climbed behind the wheel. "Best guy in town to have on your side in a time of need."

"Except he won't be on *my* side," she shouted, wanting to make that perfectly clear to everyone.

The car door slammed. Gosling drove away.

Charity looked across the dark expanse of what

seemed earlier a narrow strip of a lake and murmured, "He'll be on the *other* side."

Jason's feet shifted over the floorboards of the porch. They creaked and groaned but his low, commanding voice rose above them as he said, "No, I won't."

"You can't sleep in the cabin with me and Livie." Charity took a step toward the door. Her pulse picked up. "How would it look?"

Jason shrugged and put his foot on the top step. "I don't care how it looks."

"Well, I do." She pressed her back to the closed cabin door. "I'm a stranger to this town."

"And one who doesn't plan on staying, so that's no big deal. Besides, we're out here all on our own, who's going to know anyway?" She couldn't see his face in the darkness but she couldn't mistake the potent mingling of humor and determination in his tone.

"I'll know." She pressed her lips together and shut her eyes. "Livie would know. I've talked to her about the things that matter. To be strong in your faith and your convictions are first and foremost. There are so many times I tried to instill my values by words instead of by the way I lived my life. I won't do that now. I want to lead by example like… like…you know…"

"Like a good family does?" Jason's soft, Southern-flavored laughter washed over her. "You are so cute."

She wanted to scream that she was not cute, but that wasn't the point. The point was that the man saw straight through her and had no compunction about calling her out on her inconsistencies.

"Okay! You're right!" She went thundering down the porch steps and out onto the grassy slope in front of the old cabin, wanting to keep their voices from disturbing Livie. "It matters to me what people here think and what my family would think."

He came after her, slowly, as though he had all the time in the world.

"I'm not really as brave and independent as I make myself out to be. I'm not sure I can handle all of this on my own." She whirled around to face him. "There, I said it. Happy now?"

"It isn't a matter of me being happy, Charity," he said softly as he took her shoulders in his large, capable hands. "Or of me being right. It's a matter of me being the right kind of man to help you do whatever makes *you* happy."

His hushed words tripped over her tense nerves, drawing her skin into goose bumps. Charity swallowed to try to dispel the lump rising in her throat.

"Thanks," she whispered.

Again the sounds of the night and the lake enveloped them. Gentle waves sloshing back and forth on the shore. Frogs croaking. The branches of the trees swishing. Her own heart beating. Charity heard them all distinctly and all together like music for her ears alone.

"Tell me what I can do to help you be as brave and independent and as strong in your faith and your convictions as you need to be."

She looked out at the cabin across the way.

He made no move to follow her line of vision.

"I guess it's okay, in this special circumstance, for you to stay at the main cabin." She tried to think how they could create a private space for her and Livie apart from him. Maybe with blankets and a clothesline? "We'll find a place for you to sleep."

"I already know where I'm going to sleep." He stepped toward her.

She looked up. "You do?"

He draped his arm around her and guided her back toward the cabin and up the stairs. He put his hand on the doorknob and smiled. "I am going to sleep right here."

She tensed. "Jason, you know that—"

"On the front porch," he concluded as he anchored his feet and pointed downward.

"Front porch?" She took that news in much the same way she might feel if the man had pushed her into the lake on a hot afternoon. A little surprised. A little relieved. And with just a little bit of flailing about before she could get her bearings. "You're going to sleep outside? On the dirty old porch? With the bugs and things?"

"Sure." He turned toward the lake, his hands on his hips. "Good way to keep an eye on things and pretty convenient for tomorrow morning, too."

"Tomorrow morning?" Charity couldn't think how she'd make it through the night after that kiss, this scare and the realization that she wasn't as ready for independence as she had once believed. Now the man was talking about… "What about tomorrow morning?"

"You and I and Livie are going fishing, remember?"

"Ol' Turkey." She shut her eyes and sighed. She couldn't say no now; Livie would be counting on it and they still needed to keep up the veneer of hustle and bustle around the cabins. "Yeah, okay. We'll do that. Meanwhile, I'll go inside and get you some blankets and something to sleep on. Pink pool floatie okay?"

He grunted.

She laughed and went inside, thinking that nobody but Livie was going to get any real rest tonight.

Chapter Thirteen

A scant six hours later, she was struggling to keep her eyes open as she came out of the cabin onto the porch. The sun had not yet risen but the sky had already grown bright with the first pinks and golds of the breaking dawn.

Charity yawned and rubbed her bleary eyes. "Don't fish ever sleep in?"

Jason grinned up at her from where he sat on the bench by the door, tying his shoes. "What's the matter? Didn't sleep well last night?"

She shook her head and pretended to find the lake more interesting than the man sitting a few feet away from her. "Strange bed. Strange goings-on."

Strange emotions.

She stretched and squirmed to pull her hoodie down over her T-shirt. She hoped that dressing in layers would keep her comfy, not too hot, not too cold. With the sweatshirt over her head, she staggered forward until her foot sank down into something soft and squishy.

It wheezed.

Her breath caught in the back of her throat for only a second before she gulped in enough air to squeal and began dancing around trying to distance herself from whatever she had just stepped on, or into. "What is that? A snake? A mouse? Did I kill it?"

"No, I think it was dead already," Jason drawled.

Charity shuddered at the thought then yanked her sweatshirt down hard so she could see what had happened. Her head popped out of the neck hole and she pushed back her hair to find Jason standing before her with the pink pool floatie dangling from his pinched thumb and forefingers.

"Oh, you!" She took a swing at him but hit the deflated plastic.

"You do realize that we will be handling bait and maybe even a fish or two on this little adventure, don't you? Maybe even encounter an old tire or a rubber boot." He laughed and tossed the floatie aside. "You want to reconsider, you better do it now."

"I'll do fine," she promised as much to bolster her own confidence as to assure him. "I'm just sleepy. I just couldn't settle down out here."

"What did you expect?" he asked, way too chipper for a man who had slept on a porch on a pool floatie all night. "You've warned me more than once you have no intention of settling down here. Right?"

She didn't say a word, just went to the top of the stairs, raised her shoulders and took in a deep breath.

He came up behind her, so close she could feel his shirt rasping against the thick knit of her hoodie. "You're still dead set against staying here, right?"

She looked up and back to meet his gaze. "When you said we were going fishing, I didn't know you meant for answers."

He grinned but did not seem ready to let it go. "Maybe I'm using the wrong bait for that because the only thing I seem to be getting is—"

"Ol' Turkey better look out!" Livie came bounding onto the porch.

The door banged shut. Her shoes pounded over the weathered wooden floor, which squeaked and groaned in protest.

Livie pulled up short alongside them then wriggled her way between them before she looked up, grinned and asked at the top of her voice, "Are we going to fish off the dock?"

Charity admired the kid's timing even if she didn't completely appreciate her enthusiasm.

"I've seen pictures of kids fishing with their dads and they sit on the dock and take off their shoes and they have fishin' poles like this…" Livie took a breath while she did a quick demo of holding a fishing pole in front of her in a two-fisted grip "…and they swing their legs and laugh and eat sandwiches and—"

"Whoa." Jason stuck his hand up to create a break in the flow so he could get a word in.

But a word about what? Charity's last bit of drowsiness lifted instantly.

"First of all…" Jason began.

I am not your dad. Charity braced herself for the man who had just taken her own words a bit too literally to give her daughter a dose of the same kind of honesty.

"First of all…" he said again as he put his hands on his knees to look Livie right in the eyes. "Shh."

Livie's head and shoulders angled back away from him.

"The first rule of fishing," he whispered *loudly,* "is don't scare away the fish."

"I won't," Livie promised, wide-eyed. Then she leaned forward and asked, "What are fish *afraid* of?"

Jason busted out laughing, then put his arm around Livie's shoulders to help guide her down the steps as he said, "Us, Liv. The fish should be afraid of us."

It was a phrase that came back to haunt him an hour later after the sun had risen. The three of them sat in one of the small silver fishing boats that they'd found stored in one of the outbuildings as they cleaned up around the place. The boat bobbed and swayed slightly. Their fishing lines lay limp on top of the clear, calm water.

"I think we'd have had better luck fishing from the dock." Livie scuffed her shoes on the bottom of the boat.

"The fish do not hang out around the dock," Jason insisted. "If you want to catch them, you have to go where the fish are."

"So, we're moving?" Charity reached for the paddle.

"Very…" He looked around, first at Livie and then at the lake. "Very good idea."

Charity picked up the paddle and beamed at him. "Point the way."

"You mean you're willing to take my advice instead of charging off on your own?" he asked as he singled out a small cove close to the spot where Livie had called to them along the walking path the other day.

"What can I say?" She leaned forward to get the oar deep into the water. "I'm a sucker for a guy who listens, learns new things and isn't afraid to go after what he wants."

She gave a mighty stroke that pushed her almost all the way onto her back.

He leaned forward, his oar in the water to take his turn. "That so?"

Then back.

She took another deep plunge and together they sent the boat gliding. "Yep."

"If I'd known that, I'd have quit my job sooner and—"

"Help!" Livie's not-really-desperate, not-really-joking cry startled them both.

They dropped their paddles into the boat, not caring if the boat went drifting into the cove.

"I can't get my hook out of the water." Livie struggled, her teeth gritted, her face red.

"It's probably snagged on something." Charity winced, hoping her kid hadn't broken the equipment on a stump. Or worse, actually caught a live fish!

Jason reached for the pole but Charity gave him a sly look, asking him to let the kid try on her own first.

"Something big!" Livie called out, straining but smiling. "A fish."

"No fish is that strong," Charity said.

"Except—" Jason peered over the side of the boat into the water.

Livie leaned back, way back. Her whole face lit and her hair clung to her sweat-dampened brow. "You think I've got Ol' Turkey on the line?"

The oar in one hand, Charity reached forward with the other, her arm rigid and her fingers splayed and stiff so that she couldn't have done anything to help even if she had wanted. "Let Jason take the pole, Livie."

"No!" Jason and Livie exclaimed simultaneously.

"She can do this," he told Charity quietly. "It's just the kind of thing a person has to do for themselves."

"But what if it gets away?" Charity spoke more from wanting her child to succeed than from any desire to actually have her catch the venerable old fish.

"What if he does?" Jason met her gaze, his hand still in a white-knuckled grip on the side of the silver metal fishing boat. "You know better than anyone the lesson isn't in succeeding or failing. The real value is in having tried."

There it was. Charity released her death grip on the paddle. After so many years trying to understand Sean and this property and why his choice to anchor himself to his family had eaten away at him, Jason had just explained it in one hurried sentence. This was why she had struck out on her own, why she felt that if she let the O'Clares take care of her even a moment longer, she would be lost. Because it would make it too easy to stop trying.

"Go, Livie." Charity clamped her hand on the side of the boat. "Do whatever Jason tells you to do and give it your best."

Jason's gaze flicked upward to connect with hers. He smiled then gave her a wink.

Her heart fluttered.

"Nice and easy." He guided the child through his coolheaded words, without so much as a move to do it for her. "No quick jerking movements, pull the line and—"

Livie did as she was told and when it started to work, she looked up and asked breathlessly, "What if I do catch him? What if the first time I ever go fishing *I* catch the biggest fish in my dad's old lake?"

Charity didn't know what to say. In truth she didn't know what Livie was asking. Did she mean simply wouldn't that be cool? Or, more troubling, was she asking if that might be a sign of some sort? Or proof that Livie was just plain lucky?

They did not believe in luck. Livie knew that but in all the excitement...

Charity drew a deep breath, fearing she'd have to launch into some deep spiritual discourse right then and there.

"Wouldn't I win some kind of trophy or something?" Livie rushed on to ask.

Charity froze. "A trophy? You just want to win a trophy?"

Even as the child hung on to the pole and let the fish tire itself out, her face brightened. "There is a prize, right, Jason?"

"Well, the tournament doesn't actually start until Heritage Days next week, but for catching Ol' Turkey? You can count on some kind of reward."

"I guess we could keep him on ice for a couple days to show the tournament folks when they get out here," Charity suggested even though she didn't really want to do that.

"Okay." Livie stuck her tongue out with renewed

determination, wrestled with the pole for a moment then said, "And after I get my prize we can let him go."

The boat bobbed in the water.

Jason looked at Charity.

Charity felt ill but not because of the movement. "No, honey, to keep him on ice until the tournament he'd have to be dead."

"Dead?" Livie loosened her grip.

The reel spun.

Jason made a dive for it but Charity stopped him from intervening with a look.

Livie took control of the fishing pole again, this time with much less enthusiasm. She bit her lower lip.

Charity put her hand on Livie's back. "You kinda have mixed feelings about that, huh?"

"I don't want him to die but I sure do want a trophy." Livie frowned then looked back at her mother. "What's the right thing to do?"

Charity wanted Livie to make her own decisions but she was just a little girl and this was a grown-up kind of dilemma. If she was going to give guidance, she decided, she'd have to do with patience and wisdom, so as not to nudge the child toward a choice she would regret later.

"Don't worry, kid, if the time ever comes, you'll know," Jason spoke up before Charity could even begin to formulate her reply. "You've got a great up-bringing to lean on, a good head on your shoulders and a big heart."

Livie tugged on the pole again, suddenly aware that the fish was getting away.

Jason sat, watched and encouraged the child. "You'll do okay whatever path you—"

Snap.

The line, lure and all came flying out of the water.

Like the recoil of a whip it went sailing over their heads and out across the nearby shore and into the tall grass between the lake and the Camp Store Cabin.

Clunk.

The lure hit something. Something large and metal in a place where nothing like that should be— where nothing like that was the day Charity had gotten stuck on the path, or the day Livie had walked it or the night Deputy Gosling had patrolled it.

Jason and Charity looked at each other.

"He got away," Livie lamented.

"No," Jason said quietly as he motioned to Charity to grab her oar and work with him to get them out of the secluded cove as quickly, and quietly, as possible. "I'm afraid he didn't even try to get away."

"Huh?" Livie paused from reeling in her line.

Don't lie to my kid, she tried to tell him with a warning glance, even as she bit her lower lip hoping he also wouldn't tell her too much.

"I'm saying this is Ol' Turkey's domain, Liv. He's been here a long time."

"A year?"

"Years. Maybe more than a decade."

"So there's a fish who was here when my dad bought this place?"

"I never thought of that, but, yes, I guess so." They reached the open waters of the lake.

He reached for his cell phone then met Charity's gaze. "Battery is dead."

A car engine started.

Jason squinted at the shore, scanning, tense. "Gosling will never get here in time."

"If he comes at all," Charity said, remembering how the man had doubted they even had a problem out here.

Jason gave another deep, long stroke with his oar and moved them closer to the main cabin. Then he leaned forward on one knee to take her hand in his and command her gaze to fix in his. "Get Livie inside, lock the door then use your phone to call."

"What will you—"

He dove into the still lake water with a loud splash. The ripples he created rocked the boat.

"What's that about?" Livie wanted to know.

"That's about a man who's not afraid to try, sweetie."

"Where's he going?"

"Wherever he has to go to help us," she murmured. Then she grabbed the oars and began to row with all her might as she said, "Now we need to get to a phone and return the favor."

Chapter Fourteen

Jason only had to take a few long strokes before his foot touched lake bottom and he could pull himself up and walk. Still, he crouched low.

His heartbeat throbbed through his body. Rivulets of water over his skin gave him a chill. His lungs ached from the sudden exertion and he had to force himself to take deep, slow breaths. He made his way through the tall grass, just a few feet from the shore to the path but it seemed like it took him far too long.

He could hear the engine idling. Loud. Then louder. An old car by the sounds of it. He concentrated to try to hear if tires had begun rolling over twigs and brush.

He crept closer. Close enough that he could smell the car burning oil. It sputtered and revved, sputtered again as though struggling to keep from conking out.

It was a kid's car, he'd bet. He peered through the

grass and caught a glimpse of maroon and a dented fender. Just a kid, he decided. A kid who had scared Charity and made Livie's life seem a little less safe.

That did it, propelled him to action. He stood and shouted, "You can't get away. You might as well give up."

No response from inside the beat-up old car.

"This is where I came in," he muttered. He rubbed his hand over his eyes and pushed his wet hair off his forehead. "Only then I was dry."

And employed.

And miserable.

Jason paused; the damp lake grasses swished against his sopping wet jeans. Grass brushing over denim? He wouldn't be able to hear that unless...

"Smart move turning the engine off." He slogged through the grass a few more steps. "Make it easier for you and I to have a little talk."

"Engine's off because I ran out of gas," came a young male voice from the driver's side of the vehicle. "I don't want to talk to you."

Jason swept the back of his hand down his sopping shirt, then wicked the lake water off onto the ground. "Might as well. I'm the only one standing between you and the sheriff."

A movement made the whole car rock gently. Pine needles crunched beneath the tires. An elbow came angling out of the window in a familiar color of sweatshirt.

"USC," Jason murmured his first impression.

"I don't see any sheriff." The young man rolled his head of short, dark hair slightly to take a look in the side-view mirror.

Jason stepped around the rear bumper. His gaze fixed on the eyes in the reflection for an instant before the kid slunk down in his seat. Again, that sense of familiarity washed over him.

"Get out here," Jason bellowed. "Better to deal with me than the sheriff."

"What's the sheriff going to do?"

"How about arrest you for trespassing?" His patience was wearing thin. The kid had to know he was caught; why didn't he just give himself up? Jason had a theory about that, of course, but he didn't give away his suspicions as he folded his arms, planted his feet and told the kid, "This is private property, you know."

"I know all about this place," the kid shot back. "I have more right to be here than *you* do...*Lucky Dawg.*"

He thought so. Jason knew this kid. Or the kid knew him. Had to be local, which meant the kid had a tie to some Burdett someplace, through his younger brother's church, Josie's restaurant or maybe even a parent who worked at the Crumble. Somewhere along the line, this kid was connected to someone that Jason called "friend."

Greater love hath no man than this, that a man would lay down his life for his friends.

The verse came back to him. He had come here to

pay a debt to Sean. So much had happened that Jason had sort of lost sight of that. Bringing the law in to make a scene over some local kid would only impede Charity's efforts to sell this place, make it look like a magnet for who knew what kind of activity.

He had to figure out a better way to handle this, for Sean, for the kid and for Charity. Jason glanced over his shoulder toward the cabin. Charity and Livie had docked the boat and just headed to the cabin.

When you have to, you'll know the right thing to do.

"I don't think the sheriff will see things your way," Jason called out as he turned and strode toward the open driver's-side window.

"I've dodged that sheriff for almost a month now." In his attempt to get down low in the car, or perhaps as a show of bravado that he was completely relaxed, the kid had slid down until the back of his head rested against the edge of the open window. "He doesn't scare me."

"I see your point." Jason considered how reticent Gosling had been to actually do much of anything about the supposed intruder. "Maybe I should take it to a higher authority."

"Oh, please! Don't *you* go all churchy on me, Lucky Dawg."

"When I said higher authority, I meant me. And by the way, I don't stand for just anybody calling me…that name." The grass crackled under his footsteps. He reached for the door handle. "I only tolerate it from people I care about, people I have a long and often storied history with and—"

He jerked open the door.

The kid came spilling out, hitting the ground with a thud then a half roll that landed him flat on his back, face up.

Jason knew that face. Not from church, or Josie's or even the Crumble. He knew those eyes, that dark hair and distinct widow's peak.

"Davey O'Clare? What are you doing out here? Why didn't you let us know it was you? And most of all—"

The kid's cell phone rang and cut him off.

"Th-that's my folks." He didn't make a move to go for his phone. "They've been trying to get a hold of me for days."

Jason came up to the young man and held his hand out to help him up. "Then I suggest you answer it."

"I don't have anything to say to them." The young man used Jason's extended hand to sit up then he put his head in his hands.

"I'm sure they have plenty to say to you." Jason thought of the call Charity had taken from the boisterous couple.

"You don't understand," Davey moaned.

"A meddling family? Oh, I think I know a thing or two about those." Jason was trying to make the kid feel better and *do* better. "The best way to deal with them is to actually deal with them. Answer that call, Davey."

The phone rang again.

"I can't." He hung his head even lower. "They'll ask me stuff and I don't have any answers."

"They love you, kid." Jason couldn't believe it was him saying this, and yet he meant every word as he urged Davey, "Maybe they can help you find the answers."

"Like they helped Sean?" He looked up at last, his young face twisted with angst.

"Your parents were in no way responsible for Sean's choices." Just as the Burdetts were not to blame for the direction Jason's life had taken. "He was a man. He had options."

"I know." Davey shut his eyes. "I *know* and that only makes it worse. I flunked out last semester and they think I'm in summer school but I never even went to a single class. I'm just a big loser like my brother."

"Your brother is the reason you have to talk to your parents." Jason clenched his jaw. A thousand thoughts and emotions butted up against each other inside of him but he had to push them all aside. "They've already been through enough with Sean. If you don't answer that phone and let them know where you are and that you are safe, I will."

The kid reached for the phone.

In a matter of minutes arrangements had been made and Jason had the kid on the way to the main cabin.

Chapter Fifteen

"**D**avey O'Clare!" Charity's stomach lurched when she saw the young man dragging his feet coming up the walk alongside Jason. "You're the one behind the reports of someone lurking around out here? The one who stole from me?"

"I ran out of money." Davey, a younger, shorter, skinnier version of Sean, stopped at the bottom of the porch steps and gazed up at her. "You were going to throw those lousy mounted fish away. I just thought—"

"You did anything *but* think!" She ran both her hands back through the mass of red hair that the lake's humidity had made even thicker and curlier than normal. How could Sean's younger brother have put such a fright into her and Livie? Why wouldn't he have just come to her? "Did your parents send you here to look for me?"

"No!" Davey's dark eyes, so much like Sean's, flashed. "I came here to get away from my parents. I didn't know you'd be here. How could I? I didn't mean to scare you."

Six years younger than her and eight inches taller, she still approached the poor kid as she might someone Liv's age and size. She came down the stairs toward him, her jaw clenched and her whole body tense. "Do you have any idea how much trouble you've caused?"

"He knows." Jason stepped in to intercede. "So before you pinch him by the ear and drag him to the woodshed, I suggest you do two things."

"Calm down and call off the cops?" She glared at Jason to reinforce that she felt perfectly capable of assessing her options.

"Okay, *three* things you need to do before you tie into the kid," Jason corrected. "First, calm down."

"Don't tell me what to do!" she snapped.

"Technically, you told yourself to do that one," he shot back.

More glaring on her part. More intense than before because this time, he was right. That just irked her.

"You did, Mom," Livie chimed in.

"Good point, no matter who said it," Davey added.

They got the glare, too.

"As I was saying before I was so…adorably interrupted." Jason tried to hide his smile. "Charity, you need to calm down, call off the cops and, most importantly, you need to listen."

And learn.

The unspoken conclusion hung in the air between them.

But that was the point. Charity had learned. These past few days she had learned plenty and what good had it done her? It had only served to confuse her and muddle her objectives.

"Maybe it's your turn to listen and learn, starting with letting me finish a thought *on my own,*" Charity said to Jason before she turned to Davey, held out her arms and drew him into a deep, sincere hug. "Hey, kiddo, you really caused a lot of trouble but it is good to see you. Are you okay?"

"Yeah." He nodded and smiled sheepishly at her.

She gave his cheek a quick smack then leaned her shoulders back to get a good look at how thin and tired he appeared. "You've been sort of living by your wits around here for a while, have you?"

Another nod.

"Yeah, I can tell." She withdrew from him and rubbed her finger under her nose. "You stink."

Jason chuckled softly at what Charity considered a benevolent use of understatement.

"You hardly have room to laugh." She nailed him with a stern look and a quick sniff. "Bait, lake water, a day without a shower—not exactly the kind of scent they bottle and sell in your finer department stores."

He grinned at her.

Livie giggled. "I'm so glad everything turned out like this. Now Uncle Davey can—"

"Uncle Davey can hit the shower," Charity interrupted, slinging her arm out to show her brother-in-law the way.

He obeyed gratefully, going inside without any further comment.

"I'll show you where the bathroom is." Livie tagged along behind.

"Show him and then come back out and leave him in peace," Charity said, knowing that peace was a rarity with any O'Clare but most especially one who had gone against Jack and Kathleen's wishes. "It may take him a while to get really clean, so don't think you can hang around outside the bathroom door trying to hurry him up."

The door banged shut.

"If you're not out in one minute, I am coming in after you, Liv." Charity eased out a long breath and headed down the stairs. She needed to buy herself some time before her daughter became too invested in the idea of having her uncle around. Davey could not stay. She had enough on her plate without adding another secret to keep from the only real family she had in the world.

A family that, if they knew either she or Davey were here, would swoop in to take charge of everything.

She strolled down the slope toward the lake as though drawn to it.

"You okay?" Jason followed behind.

She'd come so far by simply coming this far. Yet now she found herself so afraid of losing her way, of repeating past mistakes, that she couldn't decide upon her next move.

Her nerves were frazzled. Her emotions raw.

This is what happens when you let yourself get distracted, that bossy voice inside her head chided.

"I'm okay," she said softly as she watched the silver boat dip and bobble where she had secured it to the shore. She thought back to that first day in the canoe. She hadn't known the basics of how to even paddle. She had feared motion sickness, loss of independence and Jason Burdett.

Now, none of that scared her. She had time to figure this out. She could still get the cabins in passable condition, put them on the market and get herself and Livie started on their new life before the O'Clares even knew she wasn't ever coming back to Pennsylvania.

She smiled at him and said again, much more confidently, "I'm definitely okay."

"Great." He made a show of taking a whiff of his shirt, frowned then nodded his head toward the rowboat. "Maybe I should go across to the other cabin and get cleaned up before—"

"You did call off the cops, right?" Davey stuck his head back out the door. "I don't want my folks to get here and find me in trouble with the law."

"Your folks?" Charity stiffened. Her stomach churned. All the old fears and anxieties came flooding back through her. "The O'Clares? Here? What do you mean?"

"I… They…" Davey came onto the porch, his expression stricken. "Jason said—"

"Grandie and Grandpop are coming?" Livie practically danced out the doorway, jumping and clapping her hands.

"I made the kid talk to the O'Clares, Charity." Jason slid his palm down her arm and took her fingers in his.

She clasped his hand. Gripped it, really. Tightly, which was just how her chest felt and exactly how her voice sounded as she demanded, "And tell them what?"

"That they might want to stay in Mt. Knott while they sorted out Davey's school problems," Jason fessed up. "I told him he had to face his family issues."

"The O'Clares? In Mt. Knott?" She didn't just drop his hand, she all but flung it away. "I suppose you told them that I was here, too?"

"I thought… Didn't they know?" He made a shrugging gesture to underscore his innocence.

"No! No, they did not know! I planned to get the cabins on the market and be gone before they even knew I was here!" She put her hand to her temple. "This is bad. This will cause a rift. They will have a thousand suggestions for what to do with these cabins, just like they have about what to do with my life, and Livie's."

"Suggestions? That's not so really bad, is it?" He let his hand drop softly on her shoulder. "You're strong, Charity, and have a mind of your own. You have your goals. They don't want to rob you of those. They love you."

"That makes it worse." She raised her arm and pushed his hand away. She jerked up her chin and fixed her eyes in his. "Don't you see that? The fact that they love me so much, that they loved Sean, only makes it all that much harder. I can't...I can't deal with it."

Her heart ached. Her head hurt. She couldn't swallow and she could just barely breathe. All her plans, all her designs to make a clean break and start over...gone. All because she let her guard down. All because of...

She turned to glower at Jason.

Davey stepped out onto the porch.

Before she could form a thought, a new plan, a means of escape, Deputy Gosling drove up and got out of his car.

"Looks like it's too late to cancel the cops." Jason held up his hand and stepped in, as he always did, to take charge. "I'll smooth things over."

Take charge.

Just like the O'Clares.

He wasn't a "go-to guy" or, as he claimed, a "get him to do it" guy. Jason Burdett was a take-charge guy.

The only problem with that was that Charity had already...finally...taken charge of her life.

"No. I'll talk to him." Charity pushed past Jason onto the porch and down the steps. When Gosling got close enough, she planted her feet, looked back at Jason and Davey and said, "Deputy, I want both these men off my property."

"What?" Jason stepped forward.

"But…the shower…" Davey whined.

"So, you called me out here to escort trespassers off your property?" Gosling looked confused.

"Yes!" Charity snapped.

"No!" Jason bellowed.

"We're not trespassers," Davey insisted. "You haven't even listened to my whole story, Charity."

"Davey, I love you like my own brother, but the truth is I don't have time for stories." Charity threw up her hands. "I ran out of time when you called your parents."

"I didn't call them, they called me and…and…and he made me take their call." Davey stabbed an accusing finger at Jason.

"It was the right thing to do," Jason spoke to Charity. "Avoiding his problems won't make them go away."

"What are you doing besides hiding out from your problems?"

"Helping you."

"How? By bringing the very people I am trying to make a clean break with right to my doorstep?"

"Clean break? That's what you call this?" He held his arms out to indicate their surrounding. "If this isn't hiding out from your problems, I don't know what is."

"I didn't come here to hide. I came here for closure so I could move on."

He paused for a moment. Then he mouthed the words *move on* before he exhaled and squinted out at the lake. After only a few seconds he shook his head and chuckled as he headed for the front steps. "I'll give you this, at least this time you didn't fling a fish at my head."

"What's going on?" Davey looked from Charity to Jason, then, anxiously at Deputy Gosling.

"You're coming with me," Jason said to the young man.

"Do you have any idea what she's talking about?" Gosling asked.

Jason met her gaze. "Yes. She's, uh, she's leaving."

"I thought *you* were leaving," the man said.

Jason didn't answer. He didn't look.

"I'm only doing this for my daughter's future," Charity called out, almost apologetically, to the man who had gotten her into this mess.

"You keep telling yourself that, Charity. One day you might even convince yourself." Jason pointed out his car to Davey and the two of them walked toward it.

"But, Mom…" Livie moved to go after them.

Charity stepped between Livie and the men, her hands on the girl's upper arms.

Neither man looked back.

Charity went up on tiptoes to make herself heard as she shouted, "I came to South Carolina as the first step in what I planned as a journey toward independence. In the past few days I've let myself get totally sidetracked. Well, no more."

Jason raised his hand in farewell but in no other way acknowledged her bold claim.

"No more Mt. Knott power breakfasts or lessons in paddling your own canoe. No more campfires or, you know, campfire-related…stuff." *No more kisses.* She exhaled and tightened her grip on Livie. With each memory she tried to dismiss, her heart grew a little heavier.

Jason did not seem to notice.

"No more stories about family dynamics, or Gravy Joe and the potato phantom," she went on, trying to make sure she got her point across.

Yeah, that's why you keep trying to push the man's buttons and get him to look back at you one more time. Now her inner voice was not just bossy, it had gone all sarcastic and unrelenting.

"Gravy Joe and the Potato Phantoms? Was that, like, a rock group in the sixties?" Gosling wondered aloud, clearly trying to make sense of her ramblings.

Jason did not give her rant that much thought. He opened his car door, and slid behind the wheel.

"No more fish called Turkey." She gave it one last effort and left no name uncalled. "No more dealing with you…you…Lucky Dawg."

"Turkey?" Gosling finally fixed every ounce of his attention on her. "You mean *Ol' Turkey?* You seen him out there?"

Jason's door slammed. Davey's, too.

"I almost caught him," Livie rushed to inform the deputy.

The car engine started.

"Really? What kind of bait did you use?" Gosling pulled a notepad from his pocket and began searching for something to write with.

"Worms." Livie shrugged then turned to her mom. "Are Jason and Uncle Davey going someplace else to take a shower? When will they be back?"

"We'll talk about all that later." Charity gave the kid a gentle nudge toward the cabin. "Right now we have to get back to work. And I'm sure there's plenty of more important things for Deputy Gosling to do, too."

"Yeah, I have to get my fishing tackle together. If Ol' Turkey is out there, I want to enter that tourney and catch that fish." He grinned at her, then tipped his ball cap and backed away. "And a word to the wise, ma'am?"

Wise? Her? Charity wanted to protest the very notion but she didn't have the strength. She tipped her head to tell him to speak his mind.

"Now that folks know the owner is on-site and Ol' Turkey's on the loose, people will start heading out to this part of the lake."

Owner on-site? That's what the man had told her

to do, be on-site. He'd told her to do it to keep people away, not to… "Wait, so because of all this, the place will get a lot of traffic?"

"I reckon so. Will you be all right with that?"

"All right?"

Try to get the place on the market in time for Heritage Days. People come from all over and you could get a quick sale. She recalled the gist of a piece of good advice a certain local hero had given her.

"That's more than all right. That just might be the answer to my prayers," she said with a refreshed smile.

He nodded, put his notepad away and left.

Charity headed into the cabin, calling, "Livie, get cleaned up. We're going into town."

Chapter Sixteen

"Family meeting. Mandatory. After church at Josie's. No excuses."

Jason had the same message in his home, his cell and his work—*ex*-work—voice mail from not one, not two but all three of his sisters-in-law.

"I am not dressing up in a cooked-up costume of some phony-baloney, probably never really existed ancestor," he had told each and every one of them.

When they each gave him a personal guarantee that the assignment of playing some "old goat on a float," as the girls had coined the job, was covered, he had relented. With three great women so happy to set his brothers up for payback for all the years of Heritage Days humiliation he had suffered, how could he not cooperate?

Besides, it wasn't like he had anything more pressing requiring his attention.

Except Davey O'Clare, who had taken up residence at Jason's home on the Burdett compound indefinitely.

And Jack and Kathleen O'Clare, who'd called every few hours for the past two days to update him on their progress in getting ready to come to South Carolina for a few days. And to tell him how to handle Davey, what to feed him, what to make him do toward getting his school problems sorted out. Then they'd usually turn their good intentions to Livie and Charity.

Even though they did not require his attention, he couldn't help but devote most of his waking—okay, and sleeping—hours to think about Livie and Charity O'Clare.

Though he'd only left the cabin forty-eight hours ago, it felt like a lifetime. Still, he knew it was the right thing to do. Give Charity room. Let her find her own course, even if it led her away from him.

He had spent his lifetime rushing to everyone's aid, real or imagined or anything in between. Now he'd fallen for the one person who did not want his help with anything.

And people had the gall to call him...

"Lucky Dawg!" Burke, Top Dawg, strolled into Josie's Home Cookin' Kitchen with his wife, Dora, bustling behind.

"Woof-woof-woo-ooo, Lucky Daw-aw-awg!" Cody, Hound Dawg, the youngest in the wolf pack hierarchy, moved with ease from his role as minister to bratty kid brother the minute he saw Jason sitting on a stool at the counter.

Josie swept past them all into the kitchen. Her son, Nathan, ran in no discernible pattern in his mom's general direction.

Cody's wife, Carol, hustled along behind, picking up toys and articles of clothing the toddler shed along the way.

"Hey, Ex-Vice President of Special Projects." Adam, Stray Dawg, clamped his beefy hand in a vise grip on Jason's shoulder. "Looks like you beat everyone here."

"Of course he did. Lone wolves travel light," Burke said as he made his way to the tables Jason had already had time to pull into one long seating arrangement when he got here after church.

"Where do you think you're going?" Adam released Jason to take a couple swaggering steps toward the chair at the head of that table, the one Burke seemed determined to take.

"Just assuming my rightful place." He pulled back the chair.

"You mean my rightful place," Adam corrected, reaching out to yank the chair in his direction.

"Actually, as your pastor..." Cody raised his hand.

The other brothers glared at him.

Cody cleared his throat. "As your pastor, I think you should both turn the other cheek."

He gave them both a nod, then, as he brushed past

Jason, muttered, "That way they would both be looking the other direction while I swiped the top spot."

Jason laughed for the first time since he'd left Twin Cabins Lake. He was glad he came today.

With his thoughts so overrun by O'Clares, Jason actually suspected his own family and their particular brand of intrusiveness might make a nice break for him. And if his two older brothers got into a wrestling match that made their wives pull rank on them both, well, that would just be the icing on the cake.

"This is family, not business. I'm the oldest. I sit at the head of the table," Burke demanded.

"We're Burdetts. Everything we do is business," Adam corrected. "I run the business so I sit—"

"Where I say you sit." Conner Burdett, tall and lean with a full head of silver-white hair and a face about as tanned and worn as saddle leather, stood in the doorway. He took a long, sweeping view of his unruly brood. "Now, the way I see it. I'm still the head of the family and the business so I'll take that chair you boys are fighting over and decide who sits on either side, got that?"

"Yes, sir," they both said.

Jason chuckled.

"You have something to add to that, Lucky Dawg?" Conner asked.

For the first time in a couple of weeks, since he'd realized the depths of his own malcontent and contemplated the role he had played in Sean's failure with the cabins, Jason found himself with his family again. For the first time since he'd quit his job, found the only woman he had ever truly loved and let her go because her happiness meant more to him than his own, Jason looked into his father's eyes.

"Yeah, I do," he said as he slipped off the stool, went to the head of the table and pulled the chair out for his father to sit in. "Don't call me Lucky Dawg anymore."

Conner stood silent for a moment.

In his eyes Jason could see he was trying to understand the request. Mainly because it had been just that. A request.

No implied threat.

No pleading.

No apologies.

"Can I ask you why not?" Conner finally asked as he lowered himself into his chair while everyone looked on with bated breath.

"Because that's not who I am," Jason answered. "I don't believe in luck. I didn't get where I am because of it and I no longer have the patience to put with any implication otherwise."

Conner paused for a moment to take that in then nodded slowly. "'Bout time, son."

Jason looked up and around to his stunned brothers.

"That got something to do with you quitting your job?" Conner wanted to know.

"Yes, sir." Jason took in a deep breath. "I think it's time I worked at something that I didn't just fall into."

Conner searched his son's face, probably thinking back to the day he had pulled Jason from the machinery and of the position given Jason at the Crumble as an adult. "Fall into…" Conner chuckled. "I like that."

Jason smiled, glad his father had not taken the remark as ingratitude nor had he taken offense at him making light of the incident that gave him his hated nickname.

"Honestly, Dad. Ever since you pulled me free from that conveyor belt as a kid I've had a hard time with that name." Jason rubbed his hand back through his hair and down his neck, feeling a bit exposed by his confession. A month ago he'd never have said a word, though, just taken it and gotten the job done. So he had to press on. "Calling me lucky made me feel as though nothing I ever did was earned, none of the many blessings I've known was deserved, just the result of dumb luck."

"No such thing as luck," Conner reminded him.

Jason shifted his feet and exhaled. "I know."

"And no blessing is ever deserved or earned. That's what makes them blessings."

"I know."

"Your only responsibility is to appreciate your blessings and be grateful."

"I…do." He did. Again, a month ago he probably couldn't have answered that way. But now? Having spent so much time with Charity and Livie? Having filled his days at the lake with hard, honest work?

Having stepped out of the shadow of his family and found himself still in the circle of their love? He did appreciate his blessings, the ones he had always had, the ones that he would only have for too brief and precious a time.

"And by the way, I was not there that day to pull you free of that belt because of luck." Conner placed his hands on the table and leaned forward to command every eye in the room. "I was there because you were there and that's where I needed to be."

Jason frowned, trying to make that almost tender sentiment fit with the harsh parent he had always thought his father to be.

"I didn't practice the warm and fuzzy brand of fatherhood with you boys." Conner scanned the crowd, making eye contact in turn with each of his sons. "I admit that. I wasn't demonstrative."

"Amen to that." Cody stood at the other end of the table, his arms crossed but wearing a smile that spoke of love and honesty.

Conner looked up at his youngest with a familiarly stern expression, which fell away the instant Cody held his father's gaze. Conner chuckled softly. "I stayed in the background. Let your mother do the hands-on stuff. But don't convince yourselves that I wasn't there, that I didn't keep my eyes on you boys."

Conner aimed a look at Cody again.

"Amen to that as well," Cody offered quietly.

"I let you boys make your own mistakes but I stayed close in case you needed me to guide you through the consequences of those mistakes, so you could learn from them."

Jason recalled Charity's determination to protect her daughter's dignity by not calling her existence a mistake. In an instant it occurred to him, though, that she never used the *mistake* word at all. He thought of her resistance to being taught a lesson. She was so wonderful. So strong and capable. What was she so afraid of? He shook his head, still unable to figure her out.

"Now, we having this family meeting or what?" Conner slapped his hands together then used the toe of his shoe to push out the chairs on either side of his seat.

The wolf pack of brothers looked at each other.

"Hound Dawg," Conner said and pointed to the seat beside his. Cody practically glowed to be so singled out. Conner pointed to the other empty seat of honor. "Lucky…that is, Jason."

"You can call me whatever you want, Dad." Jason put his hand to the chair then looked up at everyone around him. "That does not apply to the rest of y'all. I don't really care what Daddy calls me, but you are hereby given notice that I reserve the right to punch in the nose any one of you…"

"Even your pastor?" Cody interjected.

"Any one of you, including my pastor acting in

a *non*-pastoral capacity, who ever calls me that name again—"

"Sorry to interrupt Lucky Dawg, but I didn't know where else to turn." Davey came stumbling through the door of Josie's with his eyes wide and his cheeks flushed. He stopped to catch his breath.

Jason forgot all about his declaration in that moment, rushed to the kid and asked, "What's wrong? Is it Livie?"

Davey shook his head.

"Charity? Is she okay?"

"Far as I know, but I can't make any promises how long that will last."

Jason's gut twisted. "What are you talking about? Do you know about something bad that's going to happen? Do we need to get to Charity and warn her about something?"

"Warn her. Yeah, that's a good idea." He pulled up straight and gulped in a deep breath. "Someone needs to get out to the cabin and warn her that—"

The door swung open and a tall, robust couple in full USC regalia from their sandals to their sun visors crowded into the door frame.

"Davey!" the woman cried out. "There you are! You have no idea what a fright you caused us! My darlin' boy, get yourself over here and give your mother a hug!"

The man made a stiff motion with his burly arm. "Don't mind us, folks. We've come to collect our son.

Nothing to worry yourselves over, not in the least. We're just—"

"The O'Clares," Jason whispered as he looked heavenward.

"Jack and Kathleen!" Conner stood. "We're having a family get-together! Make yourselves right at home!"

"You know each other?" Jason tried to recall if he might have introduced them when he and Sean were at school. Even if he had, he concluded, there was no way his father would have recognized them, much less remembered their first names. "How?"

Conner got up and went to the couple, his hand out.

Jack and Kathleen would have none of that formality and together they wrapped the Burdetts' austere patriarch into a group hug. The couple both spoke at once, catching Conner up on their concerns about Davey and the need to see him for themselves.

"Not that we don't trust Jason. We do. No reservations at all there." Jack stepped out of the embrace and gave Jason a quick wave of acknowledgment. "In fact, of all the places on earth the boy could have landed, this was the best. Our family has good friends here in Jason and you, Conner."

Trust? Him? He had never considered for a moment they would feel that way. It surprised him almost as much as seeing his father warm to people even he thought of as strangers.

"Come, sit." Conner motioned them to the table.

The couple followed suit and took seats while Davey hung back, making a gesture that asked both "How was I to know?" and "What am I supposed to do?" that only Jason understood.

"I, uh…" Jason took a step toward the door. He had to warn Charity that her in-laws had arrived in town. Give her all the time he could to do whatever she needed to do. Whether that meant she would fortify herself or run away, he didn't know. He only knew that he had to give her the chance to meet the O'Clares on her own terms.

The rest of his family took their seats at the table.

"Carol and I will be out with pie and coffee in a minute," Josie called from the kitchen.

Jason used that distraction to move closer to the door, to making his escape.

"So, how's Sean's property?" Jack asked Conner as he settled into a chair.

Jason turned. "Why would my dad know about that?"

"Because I sublet it for years from Sean," Conner said calmly, his gaze on Jack, not on Jason.

Jack nodded slowly, appreciatively.

"He did it under a property management's name. Sean knew but we didn't." Jack did look toward Jason as he gave a few of the details. "Then after Sean…after his accident…" The man looked down for a moment to gather his composure before going on. "Your father made contact with us and let us know what he'd done. Let us know he was in a position to help again, if we needed it."

"We were so grateful for all you've done for us, Conner," Kathleen said, putting her hand on the man's arm.

"You…" Jason shut his eyes and shook his head but when he opened them again, nothing had changed—nothing made sense. "Why? You were the one who talked me out of investing in that property years ago. Why would you do that?"

"I didn't talk you out of anything," Conner protested quietly. "I told you what I thought about it."

"We all did," Burke offered and the other brothers mumbled their agreement.

"You chose, Jason. And clearly, you chose right. There was nothing out there for you. It was not your dream. If it had been, nothing I nor your brothers said would have dissuaded you from following it."

Jason didn't know what hit him harder. The unvarnished truth of all that or the fact that even back then, when Jason saw himself as undeserving and indebted to others for his blessed life, his father had already seen in him the man Jason had always hoped he would be.

"I sublet the land because it was good business, good for Mt. Knott and good for…" Conner paused and cleared his throat. "It was good for Sean. I always liked that kid and I always wished…"

"Aye, we all did," Jack murmured, his head bowed.

"We've gone over this ourselves time and again, trying to make sense of it all," Kathleen whispered. "What could we have done? What didn't we do?"

"That's what kept going through my mind at school." Davey stepped forward. "Everywhere I looked I kept thinking of Sean. I wanted someone to blame but in the end, I kept wondering how I could have made things different."

"Oh, Davey." Kathleen held her arms open wide for her only remaining child. "We all made mistakes. Most of all Sean. We can't live the rest of our lives blaming ourselves for his choices."

Davey went to his mother.

Jason watched the family close ranks and his heart ached. Ached for the loss of his good friend, ached for the waste of the blessings of what could have been an amazing life and ached that Charity and Liv were not here.

Charity could not bring herself to admit mistakes. She closed herself off to learning from them. She blamed the O'Clares for Sean's misery and wanted to escape it. Despite her insistence on that, she hadn't really thought things through beyond ridding herself of the past. But ridding herself of the past would not make it go away. Suddenly Jason knew what Charity was afraid of, and why he had to go to Twin Cabins Lake.

There was nothing out there for you. His father's words echoed back to him. Maybe not then, maybe not even a month ago, but now?

Everything Jason wanted in the world was out there and, to get it, he'd have to risk it all.

Chapter Seventeen

"Can we stop on our way out of town and buy a T-shirt like the one Jason wore?" Livie crammed the last of her things into her lavender backpack.

"It's Sunday. There probably won't be anyplace open," Charity said, suddenly glad for the timing of their departure. The last thing she wanted to carry with her into her new life was a reminder of Mt. Knott and Jason Burdett.

She zipped up her own suitcase and plunked it down on top of the folded-up air mattresses.

"Should I get my pink floatie?" Livie slung her backpack onto the floor.

"'Fraid not. Since you used it in the lake yesterday, it's sort of…" Charity gazed out the window at the early afternoon sun glinting off the bright shining water.

"Yeah, gross." Livie sighed. "I liked that floatie, though."

Charity swept her gaze around the room, to the wall where the mounted fish had hung before they rained down on Jason's head. The red-and-tan braided rug where Jason had first tackled her, thinking she was an intruder.

In a way, she supposed he'd gotten that right. She was an intruder. She did not belong in this wonderful, quiet haven from the realities of the world. Her eyes focused out the window again. "I'm going to miss it, though."

"My pink floatie?" Livie crinkled up her nose.

"No, silly, this place." Charity laughed, but it wasn't a deep, abiding kind of laugh.

"Then why do we have to leave it? This place, not my floatie," she clarified.

Charity's stomach lurched at the question. How could she stay true to her policy of never lying to her child and answer that question? How could she say she couldn't stay because it reminded her too much of all the ways Charity had failed Sean? And of how easily she had found herself attracted to a man who would always want to rush to her aid and in doing so, always make her feel like a failure at managing her own life?

Instead of that, she simply said, "Put your things in the SUV. The Realtor will be out any time now. Once I meet with her, we can be on our way."

Livie lugged her backpack to the door and looked back. "If nobody buys this place, can we come back?"

They'd probably have to. That, or go and live with the O'Clares again. Charity took in a deep breath and drew strength from the mingling scents of musty cabin, Carolina pine and lake water. "Not much chance of that, sweetie. In fact, the Realtor said she had some good news to tell us when she comes out."

"You think she sold it already?" Livie stood in the open door. With the sunlight at her back, her expression was obscured.

"Probably not but she might have had some interest or have a lead on someone who might make an offer." Charity hoped for the second. She needed to sell this place quickly for financial as well as emotional reasons. "We'll know soon enough and, after that, we're out of here for good."

"I don't think it's so good," the child muttered as she slipped out the door, letting it fall shut with a slam behind her.

Charity raised her head to call after the child. "You'll feel differently once we're in our new…"

Home? City? Routine? Hiding place?

Charity's shoulders sagged. She had no idea where they would end up or what they would do after they drove away from Mt. Knott today. She strongly suspected it would not really fix anything.

She looked around again, her eyes lighting on the fireplace where she had hung a few of the mounted fish she hadn't sold. And once again she was reminded of Jason.

Like him, she had come to this place so intricately entwined with Sean and yet so totally disconnected from him to find answers. She did not know if Jason had found any for himself. She only knew that being here had only brought her more questions.

What could she have done to help Sean find peace? How would Livie ever learn to follow her dreams when Charity's only example was running away from hers? When would her heart stop pining for those dreams that could never be, a life she could share with...

A muted pounding on the cabin door interrupted her thoughts.

Charity startled, blinked to try to bring her mind into focus then stood and put on a happy face to greet the Realtor. As she walked across the floor she said a quick prayer about the so-called good news the Realtor said she had.

"A high dollar offer, preferably cash," she added quietly, not so much as an addendum to her prayer but to keep her own thoughts upbeat and positive. In that frame of mind, she flung open the door, smiled and spoke what she wanted to hear. "Make me an offer!"

"Okay," the man standing with one arm braced against the side of the door frame said without missing a beat. "Marry me."

"Jason!" Her heart practically stopped. She stepped back into the shadow of the interior of the cabin. "I thought you were the Realtor."

"Hey, that's an improvement over a few days ago when you thought I was a criminal." He strode inside after her and shut the door. "I asked Livie to give us a minute alone, hope you don't mind."

"I…uh…" She staggered back farther still, unsure what to say or do.

"She went down to the shore." He bent to take a peek out the window and laughed. "Deputy Gosling and a few other guys are down there trying to decide how to go after Ol' Turkey. I don't know if Livie plans to give them tips on that, tell them they can use her little pink raft or order them off her property."

"Probably the last one." Another step backward until she found herself pressed against the simple table where she and Livie had taken their meals the past two days. "She's sort of feeling proprietary about that old fish."

Small talk! Why was she making small talk with this man? She should be telling him to scat, git, to hightail it out of here with his tail between his legs.

Charity pushed her hair back out of her eyes and fiddled with the top button of her bright green shirt. She'd dressed for travel today, in a linen shirt and white jeans and she realized it was probably the most presentable she'd ever been in front of Jason. Not that that mattered to her, of course, except…

Except it did matter to her.

She looked him over, obviously just come from church, all clean and handsome and yet still projecting a aura of rumpled comfort. "I don't mind about Livie but I do have a few issues with you just barging in here without warning."

"Warning? Funny you should mention..." He turned his head, pointed then walked to the fireplace. "You hung the fish back up!"

"Just a few of them." She admired her own handiwork. She hadn't been able to do much to the cabins by herself but she had cleaned them up and tried to restore the atmosphere that must have made them attractive to the corporation that had sublet them. "They are a part of this place, even though they weren't actually all caught here."

"They weren't?" He scratched his ear, then rubbed his chin, prolonging the pointless conversation in an obvious attempt to avoid telling her something. "I thought they were all Heritage Days trophy fish."

And she let him get away with his procrastination, played into it, even. Because every minute he bought by stalling, was one more minute she got to spend with him before they parted forever.

"I know you said you weren't much of a fisherman but surely you could figure out there wouldn't be that many kinds of fish in one lake?" She put her hands on her hips and forced a light smile.

"I suppose not." He frowned, studied the fish a moment longer then turned to her. "Especially the ones with dentures."

Charity smiled in earnest then. "I was actually thinking of taking that one with me."

"Not a bad idea. A woman and kid on their own, might come in handy to pack that kind of protection when you get to... Where did you say you two were headed?"

She opened her mouth, hoping her mind would readily supply the name of a likely sounding city. When it didn't she cast her gaze down and said softly, "I don't know where we're headed."

He propped his arm on the mantel like he thought he might be there a while and said, "Then maybe you ought to stay here."

"Right, and do what?" She had never worked at any one job for long but even in her varied experience, nothing had prepared her to run fishing cabins, canoe rentals or, if all else failed, work at a snack cake factory. "Marry you?"

His expression turned sober. "The offer is on the table."

"Don't be ridiculous." It *was* ridiculous. Her quickened pulse at the very prospect might belie that fact but Charity wouldn't allow an overly romantic impulse to make her an easy foil for the man's obvious joke. "We...we hardly know each other."

"Fine. So we have a long engagement," he said,

with confidence that sounded like anything but a joke. "Two, maybe three…"

She narrowed her eyes at him, waiting.

"Weeks."

She groaned. It was a joke. Good. She knew it all along. She didn't want it to be anything else, she told herself. And she didn't have time for this foolishness.

"Look, the Realtor will be here any minute then I have to meet with her and then Livie and I have to go." She shook her head. "So why don't you tell me why you came here. Jason, what do you want?"

"I just told you. To marry you."

"That was sort of cute the first time. Now it's not funny." She looked away, unwilling to let him see the hurt and confusion she knew she could not disguise. "Not one bit funny."

"It wasn't intended to be." He walked the few steps from the fireplace to where she still stood by the table. Stopping just inches away, he reached out and took one of her hands in his. "Charity, I know it has only been a few days but in those few days I've gotten to know you better, and let you get to know me better, than any other woman I've ever known."

She tugged her hand free. "Is that why you took off with Davey instead of…"

"What?" He put his hands on his hips. "Staying and fighting with you some more?"

She glared at him, mostly for calling her out on

not knowing what she really wanted of him than for suggesting she wanted any excuse to argue.

"What good would that have done, Charity?" He took her hand again, this time more lightly. So lightly that when he uncurled his fingers, her hand simply rested in his as he spoke. "You didn't want to listen to me and I didn't know what to say to you."

She looked at her small fingers against his large palm. "Has that changed?"

"For my part it has." He covered her hand with both of his. "I know what I want to say to you now, Charity."

She raised her gaze to look deeply into his eyes. "What?"

"I love you."

The world stopped. Or her heart stopped. Or maybe, probably, just for a moment, her thoughts stopped. Her fear abated. Her hopes rose. She wet her lips before asking, trying to make sure she had heard correctly, "You what?"

"Love you." He did not waver. "That's why I left with Davey, because I couldn't put my own feelings ahead of yours. That's why if after I say what I have to say to you, you still want me to go I will. But I do want to ask one thing, no matter what."

Charity braced herself. "What?"

"That you sell me this property."

"Oh, Jason." The world started up again. Her pulse thudded in her temples. The old fears and worries rushed in and overtook her hopes and dreams. She could feel the tears building and spoke quickly to try to get her thoughts out before they came. "You don't have to do that. As much as I'd love a quick turn-around on this land, I can't let you do something that monumental because of some debt you think you owe my late husband."

"I'm not offering out of a sense of indebtedness. I'm offering to buy this place for us."

"Us?" she whispered.

"Not 'us' as a couple us. I want to buy this place for myself, and I want you to sell, but only if you are selling it because it's right for you, not because you think it will release you from the past."

"It's supposed to help me create a better future for Livie and me," she protested weakly.

"If that's what you really wanted, this place wouldn't be the key to it." He dropped her hand at last and stepped back. "I know you, Charity. You are a strong and amazing woman. If you were really looking toward the future, nothing would hold you back."

"But something is holding me back," she murmured.

"Fear," he said.

"What?"

"I saw it in you because I was so familiar with it in myself." He paced toward the fireplace then back again. "Whenever I thought of how I believed I failed Sean I would repeat John 15:13. 'Greater love hath no man than this, that a man would lay down his life for his friends.' I'd go over that verse and use it as a measuring stick of my own actions and always felt I'd come up lacking."

"That's just how I feel when I think of Sean." Tears filled Charity's eyes at last. "I didn't do enough. I know I didn't."

"You loved him, Charity. That was enough."

"But if I hadn't gotten…" She sniffled, trying hard not to burst into sobs. "If I had pushed more or nagged less. If the O'Clares…"

He held his hand up to quiet her. "The O'Clares refuse to take the blame for Sean's unhappiness. They loved him and wanted the best for him but he made his own choices."

She could not look him in the eye when she nodded to let him know he had summed the family she was fleeing precisely.

"They accepted that and in doing so made you feel that you alone must be responsible for Sean's inability to get his life in order."

"Not alone." Her voice was raspy and thin from the intensity of her emotions. "I tried to blame you, too. Until I got to know you. Then I realized it was just me." A sob escaped her lips; she took a breath to hold it back then went on. "I was the one who let him down."

"No, Charity." He came to her then and put his arms around her. "If you could have, you would have laid your life down for his, but nothing you did or didn't do would have changed Sean. He had everything in life—wonderful parents, good friends, this place, you and Livie—and that wasn't enough to satisfy whatever he felt he lost by missing out on his big NFL break."

"He always had bigger dreams than any of us could give him. He deserved so much more."

"Dreams are like blessings, Charity. You don't deserve them. You appreciate the blessings. You go after your dreams. Even if you fail, you count that as its own kind of blessing, that you tried."

She nodded. It all seemed so clear now. "Sean stopped trying."

"It wasn't your fault. Or mine."

"But I keep thinking about the accident…"

"His death *was* an accident. No one is to blame for that. His life? That was his choice. You couldn't change that. But you can change what happens next."

"How?" she asked quietly, turning away.

Marry me. How she longed for him to ask it again.

"I…well, I guess it's what Livie said a couple of days ago. Point yourself in the direction you want to go and paddle your own canoe."

"Point yourself in the direction you want to go and paddle your own canoe," she murmured. "Good advice."

She faced him and in doing so finally, after so much time living in fear and anguish, faced herself. In that instant she finally saw the future of her dreams. "Make me an offer."

He frowned, looked down, stroked his chin and then made a vague gesture with his hand as he said, "Okay, whatever your Realtor said it's worth plus—"

"No. Not for the property. The property is no longer on the market. But I am." She stepped close, put her hands on his chest and looked up into his eyes at last. "Make me that offer you did when I opened the door. I have my answer now."

"Marry me?"

"Yes. But I do think we should have a proper engagement," she hurried to say just as he bent to kiss her.

"Mom! The Realtor is... Whoa!" Livie burst through the door and pulled up short. "Does this mean what I think it means?"

"Yep," Charity said, her gaze still locked in Jason's. "Tell her the property isn't for sale anymore. We're staying."

"Yippee!" Livie leaped in the air like any kid who had just had her dream come true would, but when her feet touched the ground again she went all mature and proper. "I'm only going to leave you two alone now for a minute, so don't think you can keep kissing all day."

Jason laughed then, as the child disappeared, asked, "Does that mean we can keep kissing at least part of the day?"

"Yes, but don't get any wild ideas." She gave a nod toward the trophies over the fireplace. "Remember I have a fish with your name on it and I'm not afraid..."

"Leave it at that."

"Yeah. I am not afraid. Not of the future. Not of the past."

"That's a blessing for which I will always be grateful."

They kissed at last and when they parted, Livie ran in again to announce that the O'Clares had just driven up. Charity didn't even flinch.

Epilogue

Heritage Days, Day One
Kickoff Parade

"**Y**ou ready to go?" Jason stood in the front doorway of his Irish cottage–style house on the Burdett
compound to call for Livie and Charity.

They had decided to keep the news of their engagement quiet until after the Heritage Days chaos.
By then the O'Clares would have gone home and
Davey would have settled into his new job working
at the Crumble factory by day and helping Jason get
the old cabins ready for rental in his free time.

Because he was spending so much time at the
lake, Jason had suggested that Charity and Livie
move into his home while he and Davey stayed at
Twin Cabins Lake. He liked the idea of Charity in his
home and looked forward to the day they would

share it with Livie and hopefully a few tiny blessings of their own.

But right now the parade awaited.

"C'mon, you two. I want to get to Josie's before any of my brothers do," he called again.

"Just a sec." Charity stuck her head out from the kitchen door to speak to him, did a double take then laughed and asked, "Who or *what* are you supposed to be?"

He held out his arms in his tie-dyed T-shirt, patched jeans and leather headband. "I'm Gravy Joe."

"Gravy…I thought that was a distant ancestor!"

"Ancestor? Eh, more like an uncle. But as for distant? Man, he was far out."

Charity groaned. "You mean the guy who had all the land your family business is on was…?"

"My mother's uncle. My mom's family was loaded, and I mean with moncy," he was quick to add. "So, you two ready to go or not?"

"We're ready." The two of them stepped into the main room all done up in crazy costumes. "Ta-da!"

Jason laughed to see them all done up but had to say, "You didn't have to dress up, you know."

"I know, but you said Heritage Days are a celebration of the past. And so I thought…" She did a quick turn in her green outfit with a plastic potato toy bobbling on her head. "Get it?"

"The Potato Phantom?" He laughed. "It's perfect."

"Hey, Sean always said that's what brought our families from Ireland."

"Great tribute to them and nod to Sean as well." He held his hand out to her.

"And me!" Livie jumped up and waved around a cardboard placard. "Don't forget me! What do you think I am?"

"No trespassing?" He read the sign aloud then looked at her blue and green outfit with paper fins pinned to it. "You're one of those trophy fish who doesn't want any visitors?"

"No! I'm Ol' Turkey! And I don't want anyone to come around and catch me. Not in our part of the lake anyway!"

"Okay, let's go, then. But I warn y'all, dressed like this it might be harder than you think to keep people from guessing we're soon going to be our own little family," he warned them.

"What do you mean?" Charity asked as she hustled her child toward Jason's car.

"Well, look at us. Turkey, potatoes and gravy? Anyone could see that we belong together."

Charity laughed and gave him a kiss before she got in the car.

Livie giggled and as the two of them walked to the other side she took his hand and looked up at him. She didn't say a word, but like her mom she didn't have to.

That look said it all. For all the things he had done in his life he had finally achieved the one thing that he deserved the least and loved the most. He was somebody's hero.

* * * * *

Dear Reader,

It was so nice to go back to Mt. Knott again, this time to give the last lone wolf from the Burdett pack of brothers a romance of his own. I loved the setting this time, not in the town itself but in the mountains on a serene lake. It was a little like taking a vacation myself, writing about old friends and getting to remember my days as a camp counselor (at Central Christian Camp in Guthrie, Oklahoma), canoeing and sitting around the campfire. That always has its own kind of romance for me, and has been such a wonderful way of seeing God in nature. So I wanted to give Jason Burdett and Charity O'Clare that same sense of wonder and a place in which their love could grow.

I also loved being able to revisit the Burdett family to share their love of one another and the Lord with them and those who have enjoyed reading about them.

Thank you for letting me do that!

Annie Jones

QUESTIONS FOR DISCUSSION

1. What person do you most look up to as a hero?

2. Jason felt guilt over the many good things in his life he felt he had not deserved or worked for. If you could give him advice about that feeling, what would you say?

3. Charity feels she must make a complete break to get a fresh start in life. Do you think she would have succeeded in both making the break and starting over without any family support?

4. How did you feel about Charity's policy of honesty with Olivia?

5. The verse that Jason recalled when thinking of Sean spoke of the greatest love for a fellow man. Jason felt this applied not just to his actual life but that he should have been willing to sacrifice everything for another. Do you agree with this interpretation?

6. Do you think that if Jason had become Sean's partner in the tourist cabin business that they

both would have been better off? Or would they both still have had a lot to work out?

7. Charity loved Mt. Knott for its sense of community. This was not just about the town but about the Burdett family, the people who wrote on the board at Josie's restaurant and the people who had fond memories of Twin Cabins Lake. What groups give you a sense of community and how important are they to your contentment in life?

8. If you had caught Ol' Turkey, would you have thrown him back or gone for the trophy? Explain your answer.

9. Charity and Jason both felt the impact of their meddling families on their lives, yet they loved them and needed them. Many Christian families maintain close ties through the generations. How do you think families can find the right balance so that they are supportive and not intrusive?

10. The characters in this book fell in love quickly, though they had a history. Do you think whirlwind romances are only the kind of thing that works out in fiction, or is it a real way for some marriages to start and flourish?

11. Are you somebody's hero? Who is your hero and why?

12. Would you want to live in a town like Mt. Knott? Why or why not?

Turn the page for a sneak preview of
bestselling author
Jillian Hart's novella
"Finally a Family."

One of two heartwarming stories celebrating
motherhood in
IN A MOTHER'S ARMS.

On sale April 2009, only from
Steeple Hill Love Inspired Historical.

Chapter One

Montana Territory, 1884

Molly McKaslin sat in her rocking chair in her cozy little shanty with her favorite book in hand. The lush new-spring green of the Montana prairie spread out before her like a painting, framed by the wooden window. The blue sky was without a single cloud to mar it. Lemony sunshine spilled over the land and across the open window's sill. The door was wedged open, letting the outside noises in—the snap of laundry on the clothesline and the chomping crunch of an animal grazing. My, it sounded terribly close.

The peaceful afternoon quiet shattered with a crash. She leaped to her feet to see her good—and only—china vase splintered on the newly washed wood floor. She stared in shock at the culprit standing at her other window. A golden cow with a white blaze down her face poked her head farther across the sill. The bovine gave a woeful moo. One look told her this was the only animal in the yard.

"And just what are you doing out on your own?" She set her book aside.

The cow lowed again. She was a small heifer, still probably more baby than adult. The cow lunged against the sill, straining toward the cookie racks on the table.

"At least I know how to catch you." She grabbed a cookie off the rack and the heifer's eyes widened. "I don't recognize you, so I don't think you belong here."

Molly skirted around the mess on the floor and headed toward the door. This was the consequence of agreeing to live in the country, when she had vowed never to do so again. But her path had led her to this opportunity, living on her cousin's land and helping the family. God had quite a sense of humor, indeed.

Before she could take two steps into the soft, lush grass surrounding her shanty, the cow came running, head down, big brown eyes fastened on the cookie. The ground shook.

Uh-oh. Molly's heart skipped two beats.

"No, Sukie, no!" High, girlish voices carried on the wind.

Molly briefly caught sight of two identical school-aged girls racing down the long dirt road. The animal was too single-minded to respond. She pounded the final few yards, her gaze fixed on the cookie.

"Stop, Sukie. Whoa." Molly kept her voice low and kindly firm. She knew cows responded to kindness better than to anything else. She also knew they were not good at stopping, so she dropped the cookie on the ground and neatly stepped out of the way. The cow skidded well past the cookie and the place where Molly had been standing.

"It's right here." She showed the cow where the oatmeal treat was resting in the clean grass. While the animal backed up and nipped up the goody, Molly grabbed the cow's rope halter.

"Good. She didn't stomp you into bits," one of the girls said in serious relief. "She ran me over real good just last week."

"We thought you were a goner," the second girl said. "She's real nice, but she doesn't see very well."

"She sees well enough to have found me." Molly studied the girls. They both had identical black braids and golden-hazel eyes and fine-boned porcelain faces. One twin wore a green calico dress with matching sunbonnet, while the other wore blue. She recognized the girls from church and around town. "Aren't you the doctor's children?"

"Yep, that's us." The first girl offered a beaming, dimpled smile. "I'm Penelope and that's Prudence. We're real glad you found Sukie."

"We wouldn't want a cougar to get her."

"Or a bear."

What adorable children. A faint scattering of freckles dappled across their sun-kissed noses, and there was glint of trouble in their eyes as the twins looked at one another. The place in her soul thirsty for a child of her own ached painfully. She felt hollow and empty, as if her body would always remember carrying the baby she had lost. For one moment it was as if the wind died and the earth vanished.

"Hey, what is she eating?" One of the girls tumbled forward. "It smells like a cookie. You are a bad girl, Sukie."

"Did she walk into your house and eat off the counter?" Penelope wanted to know.

The grass crinkled beneath her feet as the cow tugged her toward the girls. "No, she went through the window."

Penelope went up on tiptoe. "I see them. They look real good."

Molly gazed down at their sweet and innocent faces. She wasn't fooled. Then again, she was a soft touch. "I'll see what I can do."

She headed back inside. "Do you girls need help getting the cow home?"

"No. She's real tame." Penelope and the cow trailed after her, hesitating outside the door. "We can lead her anywhere."

"Yeah, she only runs off when she's looking for us."

"Thank you so much, Mrs.—" Penelope took the

napkin-wrapped stack of cookies. "We don't know your name."

"This is the McKaslin ranch," Prudence said thoughtfully. "But I know you're not Mrs. McKaslin."

"I'm the cousin. I moved here this last winter. You can call me Molly."

Penelope gave her twin a cookie. Beneath the brim of her sunbonnet, her face crinkled with serious thought. "You don't know our pa yet?"

"No, I only know Dr. Frost by reputation. I hear he's a fine doctor." That was all she knew. Of course she had seen his fancy black buggy speeding down the country roads at all hours. Sometimes she caught a brief sight of the man driving as the horse-drawn vehicle passed—an impression of a black Stetson, a strong granite profile and impressively wide shoulders.

Although she was on her own and free to marry, she paid little heed to eligible men. All she knew of Dr. Sam Frost was that he was a widower and a father and a faithful man, for he often appeared very serious in church. She reached through the open door to where her coats hung on wall pegs and worked the sash off her winter wool.

Prudence smiled. "Our pa's real nice and you make good cookies."

"And you're real pretty." Penelope was so excited she didn't notice Sukie stealing her cookie. "Do you like Pa?"

"I don't know the man, so I can't like him. I suppose I can't dislike him either." She bent to secure the sash around Sukie's halter. "Let me walk you girls across the road."

"You ought to come home with us." Penelope grinned. "Then you can meet Pa."

"Do you want to get married?" Penelope's feet were planted.

So were Prudence's. "Yes! You could marry Pa. Do you want to?"

"M-marry your pa?" Shock splashed over her like icy water.

"Sure. You could be our ma."

"And then Pa wouldn't be so lonely anymore."

Molly blinked. The words were starting to sink in. The poor girls, wishing so much for a mother that they would take any stranger who was kind to them. "No, I certainly cannot marry a perfect stranger, but thank you for asking. I would take you two in a heartbeat."

"You would?" Penelope looked surprised. "Really?"

"We're an awful lot of trouble. Our housekeeper said that three times today since church."

"Does your pa know you propose on his behalf?"

"Now he does," a deep baritone answered. Dr. Frost marched into sight, rounding the corner of the shanty. His hat brim shaded his face, casting shadows across his chiseled features, giving him an even more imposing appearance. "Girls! Home! Not another word."

"But we had to save Sukie."

"She could have been eaten by a wolf."

Molly watched the good doctor's mouth twitch. She couldn't be sure, but a flash of humor could have twinkled in the depths of his eyes.

"You must be the cousin." He swept off his hat. The twinkle faded from his eyes and the hint of a grin from his lips. It was clear that while his daughters amused him, she did not. "I had no idea you would be so young."

"And pretty," Penelope, obviously the trouble-maker, added mischievously.

Molly's face heated. The poor girl must need glasses. Although Molly was still young, time and sadness had made its mark on her. The imposing man had turned into granite as he faced her. Of course he had overheard his daughters' proposal, so that might explain it.

She smiled and took a step away from him. "Dr. Frost, I'm glad you found your daughters. I was about ready to bring them back to you."

"I'll save you the trouble." He didn't look happy. "Girls, take that cow home. I need to stay and apologize to Miss McKaslin."

She was a "Mrs." but she didn't correct him. She had put away her black dresses and her grief. Her marriage had mostly been a long string of broken dreams. She did better when she didn't remember. "Please don't be too hard on the girls on my behalf. Sukie's arrival livened up my day."

"At least there was no harm done." He winced. "There was harm? What happened?"

"I didn't say a word."

"No, but I could see it on your face."

Had he been watching her so closely? Or had she been so unguarded? Perhaps it was his closeness. She could see bronze flecks in his gold eyes, and smell the scents of soap and spring clinging to his shirt. A spark of awareness snapped within her like a candle newly lit. "It was a vase. Sukie knocked it off my windowsill when she tried to eat the flowers, but it was an accident."

"The girls should take better care of their pet." He drew his broad shoulders into an unyielding line. He turned to check on the twins, who were progressing down the road. The wind ruffled his dark hair. He seemed distant. Lost. "How much was the vase worth?"

How did she tell him it was without price? Perhaps it would be best not to open that door to her heart. "It was simply a vase."

"No, it was more." He stared at his hat clutched in both hands. "Was it a gift?"

"No, it was my mother's."

"And is she gone?"

"Yes."

"Then I cannot pay you its true value. I'm sorry."

His gaze met hers with startling intimacy. Perhaps a door was open to his heart as well, because sadness tilted his eyes. He looked like a man with many regrets.

She knew well the weight of that burden. "Please, don't worry about it."

"The girls will replace it." His tone brooked no argument, but it wasn't harsh. "About what my daughters said to you."

"Do you mean their proposal? Don't worry. It's plain to see they are simply children longing for a mother's love."

"Thank you for understanding. Not many folks do."

"Maybe it's because I know something about longing. Life never turns out the way you plan it."

"No. Life can hand you more sorrow than you can carry." Although he did not move a muscle, he appeared changed. Stronger, somehow. Greater. "I'm sorry the girls troubled you, Miss McKaslin."

Mrs., but again she didn't correct him. It was the sorrow she carried that stopped her from it. She preferred to stand in the present with sunlight on her face. "It was a pleasure, Dr. Frost. What blessings you have in those girls."

"That I know." He tipped his hat to her, perhaps a nod of respect, and left her alone with the restless wind and the door still open in her heart.

* * * * *

Don't miss IN A MOTHER'S ARMS.
Featuring two brand-new novellas
from bestselling authors
Jillian Hart and Victoria Bylin.
Available April 2009
from Steeple Hill Love Inspired Historical.

And be sure to look for SPRING CREEK BRIDE
by Janice Thompson,
also available in April 2009.

REQUEST YOUR FREE BOOKS!

2 FREE INSPIRATIONAL NOVELS
PLUS 2
FREE
MYSTERY GIFTS

YES! Please send me 2 FREE Love Inspired® novels and my 2 FREE mystery gifts (gifts are worth about $10). After receiving them, if I don't wish to receive any more books, I can return the shipping statement marked "cancel". If I don't cancel, I will receive 4 brand-new novels every month and be billed just $4.24 per book in the U.S. or $4.74 per book in Canada, plus 25¢ shipping and handling per book and applicable taxes, if any*. That's a savings of over 20% off the cover price! I understand that accepting the 2 free books and gifts places me under no obligation to buy anything. I can always return a shipment and cancel at any time. Even if I never buy another book, the two free books and gifts are mine to keep forever.

113 IDN ERXA   313 IDN ERWX

Name	(PLEASE PRINT)	
Address		Apt. #
City	State/Prov.	Zip/Postal Code

Signature (if under 18, a parent or guardian must sign)

Order online at www.LoveInspiredBooks.com

Or mail to Steeple Hill Reader Service:

IN U.S.A.: P.O. Box 1867, Buffalo, NY 14240-1867
IN CANADA: P.O. Box 609, Fort Erie, Ontario L2A 5X3

Not valid to current subscribers of Love Inspired books.

Want to try two free books from another series?
Call 1-800-873-8635 or visit www.morefreebooks.com

* Terms and prices subject to change without notice. N.Y. residents add applicable sales tax. Canadian residents will be charged applicable provincial taxes and GST. Offer not valid in Quebec. This offer is limited to one order per household. All orders subject to approval. Credit or debit balances in a customer's account(s) may be offset by any other outstanding balance owed by or to the customer. Please allow 4 to 6 weeks for delivery. Offer available while quantities last.

Your Privacy: Steeple Hill Books is committed to protecting your privacy. Our Privacy Policy is available online at www.SteepleHill.com or upon request from the Reader Service. From time to time we make our lists of customers available to reputable third parties who may have a product or service of interest to you. If you would prefer we not share your name and address, please check here. ☐

LIREG08R

Everyone in Mule Hollow
can see the resemblance
between former Texas
Ranger Zane Cantrell and
Rose Vincent's son. Zane
is in shock—how could
Rose have kept such a
secret from him? Rose
reminds Zane that *he's*
the one who walked away.
Zane needs to convince her
he had had no choice…
and that's when the
matchmaking begins.

Look for

Texas Ranger Dad
by
Debra Clopton

*Available April
wherever books are sold.*

**Steeple
Hill®**

LI87524

Love Inspired®

TITLES AVAILABLE NEXT MONTH
Available March 31, 2009

TWICE UPON A TIME by Lois Richer
Weddings by Woodwards

Between his work and his twin boys, widower Reese Woodward has no time for love. Or so he thinks until he meets Olivia Hastings, his sister's best friend. Her past makes her wary of romance, but who can resist the adorable twins—or their father? Together they might find their second chance for a doubly blessed happy-ever-after.

TEXAS RANGER DAD by Debra Clopton
A Mule Hollow Novel

When Texas Ranger Zane Cantrell returns to Mule Hollow after years away, he comes face-to-face with the son of an old girlfriend—who also happens to be his son! Zane can't believe Rose Vincent kept this secret from him all these years. But he's eager to get to know his boy, and to prove he's never stopped loving Rose. Can they build a brand-new life together?

HOMECOMING BLESSINGS by Merrillee Whren

Small-town girl Amelia Hiatt and big-city businessman Peter Dalton think they have nothing in common. When they team up on a special project, they soon realize they're more alike than they could ever imagine. Except the big-city bachelor isn't ready to settle down, and Amelia is ready for a family of her own. But she's determined to change his mind—and his heart.

READY-MADE FAMILY by Cheryl Wyatt
Wings of Refuge

Ben Dillinger is used to playing the hero to damsels in distress, he's just not used to falling in love with them! When the pararescue jumper rescues single mom Amelia North and her daughter from a car accident, Ben realizes he's found the family he's been longing for. And he'll do whatever it takes to prove to her that he's the missing piece in her ready-made family.

LICNMBPA0309